L. Haren

A
Holiday Year

A
Holiday Year

A Novel by
C. G. Draper

Little, Brown and Company
Boston Toronto

First Edition

A section of this book is based on the short story "The Secret," which was published in the Spring 1975 *Prairie Schooner*. Copyright a 1975 University of Nebraska Press.

The characters and events portrayed in this book are fictitious. Any similarities to real persons, living or dead, are coincidental and not intended by the author.

Library of Congress Cataloging-in-Publication Data
Draper, C. G.
  A Holday year: a novel / by C.G. Draper.
    p. cm.
  Summary: Ned celebrates each holiday throughout the year in a memorable fashion.
  ISBN 0-316-19203-1
  [1. Holidays — Fiction. 2. Family life — Fiction. 3. Humorous stories.] I. Title.
PZ7.D78318Ho 1988
[Fic] — dc19   87-31008
                                                          CIP
                                                           AC

10 9 8 7 6 5 4 3 2 1

FG

Published simultaneously in Canada
by Little, Brown & Company (Canada) Limited

Printed in the United States of America

With love and gratitude
to our parents

George and Sophie Carter Whitin Draper
Richard Merrill and Jeannette McGrail Whitney

Contents

The Halloween Geek
1

The Thanksgiving Turkey
25

The Christmas Secret
49

The Valentine Daze
77

The Passover Easter
101

The Fabulous Fourth
125

The Halloween
Geek

THE HALLOWEEN PARTY needed one last finishing touch. I took some old jeans and a woolen shirt of Dad's, and stuffed them with rags. When the scarecrow body was ready, I leaned it up next to the barn door. Then I put a carved pumpkin on top for a head, and Mom's old gardening hat on top of that. The scarecrow was big and crooked. I thought it looked terrific. My little sister, Sally, and her friends would walk right by it on their way into my Patented House of Horrors.

I walked back down the hill to our house feeling great. Mom and Dad were paying me to run Sally's Halloween party, and so far the job had been a piece of cake. We've got this old barn up the hill from our house, and my buddy, Vic Wyluda, had helped me fix it up. Magic is my hobby, so first we made a Theater of Magic in the middle of the floor, where I would do my tricks. Then in the old horse stalls nearby we set up the masterpiece: Scream Your Guts Out. That's what the kids would do when I blindfolded them and made them feel stuff like the peeled grapes I'd say were eyeballs, and the warm tomato juice I'd say was vampire's blood, and the cold greasy spaghetti I'd say was worms gathered on a new grave at midnight.

Then there was the Black Widow Spider's Web. It was a whole bunch of fishing lines tangled up like cobwebs back and forth over a couple of the old horse stalls. At the end of each line was a prize, a plastic pumpkin filled with candy corn. Each kid would take the end of one line, and they'd have to climb all over each other untangling the lines until they got to their prizes.

Finally there was the Walk to Terror. I was going to blindfold the kids again and lead them up the rickety stairs to the hayloft, where I'd tell them they had to walk the plank over the Deep Pit of Hell, even though the "bridge" was only about two inches off the floor. Then I'd lead them all the way down to the barn cellar, where there was a lot of rich-smelling earth, and I'd tell them they would be buried alive there unless they screamed like crazy. Of course they'd all scream like crazy, because little kids love to scream. It was really going to be great.

So I felt good when I got home for dinner, and even better that Mom had fixed my favorite food, big hamburgers. We don't get them much because Mom usually cooks weird foreign things. My older sister, Pat, had mashed some potatoes — that's her specialty — and they were swimming in butter. There were frozen peas, too — a great meal on a great evening. I should have known it was too good to last.

The bomb dropped just after Dad served us all and asked how the party plans were coming. Pat began talking to Sally about the party food. She was going to help me and Victor give the kids hot dogs and cider and stuff right at the start before she went off to her Halloween dance at school.

"Do you think the hot dogs will get cold on the way up to the barn?" Sally asked.

"Do you think anyone will care?" I answered.

"By the way, Sally," Mom said, smiling brightly and talking fast, as if she wasn't totally changing the subject, "did I tell you that Uncle Harry and Aunt Michelle are coming tomorrow? And your cousin Henri, too, of course."

There was a total silence for a split second while we all stopped in our tracks. Then Sally dropped her fork accidentally on purpose.

"Not to *my* party!" she said. Sally's the kind of skinny little kid who always says exactly what's on her mind.

"Well, no, dear, of course not. Not as one of your guests, no. After all, he's Ned's age. But he can certainly help Pat and Ned with the food and things."

Now Mom was talking in that slow voice she uses when she wants everybody to be friends.

"But you said Vic could help," I said. "We've got everything set up perfect. Henri will mess it up; I know he will. Pat, we don't need him, right?"

Pat put down her fork. She lifted her hands and made that face where you pull your eyes out to slits and squash your nose up like a pig. Then she said in a fake French accent, "No, of courrse not, 'enri-de-eye weel be no help. He ees a beeg fat clomsy dees-gusting geek!"

Cousin Henri moved here from Canada about a year ago. We call him 'enri-the-eye because he spells his name with an *i* (and can't pronounce the *h*), and because he has one strange eye that doesn't focus, so he never seems to look right at you. Mom says it's called a walleye. But it's not even how he looks that gets us. It's the way he chews with his mouth open, and dribbles, and picks his nose, and laughs too hard at his own dumb jokes.

Sally almost choked on her milk laughing at Pat, but Dad didn't think it was funny. "Pat!" he said, frowning. "I'm surprised you feel that it's amusing to mock a newcomer's English. I suppose your French pronunciation is perfect?"

So Pat shut up and we all began to eat. It was quiet, and I could feel Mom and Dad giving each other looks, and then Dad said, "Speaking of Halloween, did I ever tell you about your Great-uncle Harwood's costume? That's Grandmother Scott's brother. Best getup I ever saw, and I was your age. Harwood hired a hearse and a coffin, and six men dressed as pall-bearers carried him to a party dressed as the corpse. When they set down the coffin, Harwood rose from the dead, painted a ghastly white, covered with worms!"

Dad has a way of trying to cheer us up when we're bummed by telling stories about his weird relatives. Sometimes it works, but tonight all that happened was that Sally said, "Gross. That's the kind of thing Henri would probably do. He'll do anything to get attention."

"Oh, come now," Mom said. "Henri is family. You know he hasn't had time to make many friends in this country. Is it so hard for you to show him some kindness?"

"I don't see why everybody in this family has to be so weird," Sally complained, stirring her peas into her mashed potatoes.

"But what about Vic?" I said to Mom. "You said I could have him to help with the party."

"Don't whine, Ned," Dad said. "Of course Vic is welcome to come."

Not with Henri here, I said to myself.

More silence.

So dinner was no joy, even though the hamburgers were good. Afterwards I called Vic and told him he might as well stay home the next night. Then

I went to my room to practice my magic tricks, which I had been doing all week so that I almost flunked a math test and my book report wasn't even started — in fact the *book* wasn't even started. And halfway through the four red balls trick, Sally came in and jumped on my bed, and the balls and shells went everywhere.

"Sorry," she said. "But listen. About Henri? Ned, I really don't want him at the party. You know at the Labor Day picnic, when you went off on that boat? He kept pulling Sabina's tail, and then he lifted her up by it, and when she scratched him he kicked her. Hard."

"Like I say, he's a geek," Pat said, coming in and sitting down backwards on the desk chair. "He smells like a pig."

"He likes to give you little punches," I said. "Like, he'll say something really dumb and obvious, and then if you don't say anything back, he gives you this little punch on the arm and says 'Eh?' and then laughs like a loon." I gave Sally a little punch on her arm. "Eh?" I said. Punch. "Eh? Har, har, har." Punch.

"Okay, okay, I *get* it," she said.

"Maybe you can get Vic Wyluda to deep-six him from the hayloft," Pat said.

"Come off it, Pat," I said. "I wouldn't subject a friend to Henri's company. Henri's too dumb, he's too big and blobby. He's weird, he's mean, he never looks at you, he's a geek and a ghoul and a total jerk, okay?"

"Gee, Ned, you don't seem very fond of your cousin," Pat said. She began to laugh, and said in her best Mom-like voice, "Is it so hard for you to show him some kindness?"

Sally started giggling, and finally I had to laugh, too.

But I wasn't exaggerating. The very next day, Halloween, I was in my bedroom doing one final run-through of my magic show. My door was open, but my back was to it, so I didn't hear Henri come up behind me. I'm not very big for my age, and when Henri hit me from behind, it felt like I was being tackled by a guard on the New England Patriots. He threw an arm around my chest and we pitched forward halfway across the bedroom.

"Boo!" he said as once again the four-red-balls trick went all over the room. I elbowed him off me and turned to face him. His big round head looked like a pumpkin. He stood there big and blobby, his right eye looking somewhere to my left.

"Boo!" he said again with his dumb laugh. " 'Alloween, eh? Har, har, har."

I got down on the floor to pick up my red balls and shells. "What are you doing?" he said. "Magic, right?"

"That's right."

"Practicing, I bet. For Sally's party, eh?"

"Right again," I said.

"Then you teach me a couple of tricks," he said. "I'll do them for the little ones. Your mother said I could."

I stood up and looked at him. I couldn't believe Mom had told him he could butt in on my magic.

" 'Enri 'Oudini," he said. "Eh? 'Enri 'Oudini?"

I was thinking, geez what a *ghoul*, but I should have been answering him, because he suddenly punched me hard on the shoulder. "What do you think? 'Enri 'Oudini? Har, har, har."

"Okay, fine: Henri Houdini. Now let's get started," I said.

I was going to have to give him something to do. I sat him down in the desk chair so he couldn't punch me, and I taught him the two easiest tricks I had: the Handkerchief Hat and the Disappearing Wand. They are good tricks that you can buy through the mail, and they don't need a lot of sleight-of-hand. In one, you show the audience an empty hat and then you pull a lot of colored handkerchiefs out of it, and in the other you make a magic wand disappear into the hat. I thought even Henri could learn to do them okay.

After he practiced them awhile I took him up to the barn to show him how everything was set up. We passed by the kitchen on the way and got apples; Henri chowed his down in three slobbering bites, but it was up at the barn that he really started to get to me.

First, he began shadowboxing with my scarecrow and accidentally knocked the pumpkin head off, and it cracked, but in back so you couldn't see it — as Henri kept pointing out. Then he pulled out some matches to light the candles in the jack-o'-lanterns Mom and Sally had made, and I told him how Dad never even allowed matches in the old barn, and Henri said that was kid stuff. When I showed him the Black Widow Spider's Web he waded right into it and snapped two of the lines, and I had to pull him off. In Scream Your Guts Out, he began feeling all the gross things and giggling worse than a kid. Finally I had to yell at him.

"Henri!" I said. "Look. If you're going to help with this thing, then you've got to do it my way or not at all."

He just shrugged and looked someplace over my head.

"I mean it," I said. "You want to help or not?"

He gave me a grin that looked like a smirk. "If you want me to," he said, his eyes sort of rolling toward the walls.

I had to clamp my mouth shut. *Want* him to? Yeah, about as much as I wanted a kick in the gut. But since I had to have him, I figured I'd put him where he'd do the least amount of damage. I thought the Walk to Terror would be safe, so I showed him the route upstairs to the hayloft, across the Deep Pit of Hell plank, then down to the barn cellar. He really liked the cellar, especially when I told him that's where they used to shovel out manure. There was one small light bulb down there which gave just enough light so you could see the real spiderwebs and the mounds of dark earth. It was just like a graveyard. I showed Henri the paper bag where I was keeping the poisoned mushrooms (actually marshmallows) that he was supposed to feed the kids before telling them to scream like crazy. He stuffed about six of them into his mouth before I could stop him.

"Poisoned, eh?" he said with his mouth full. Then he reached down and got a handful of black manure dirt and held it up to his mouth like he was going to eat that, too.

"Henri, will you cut it out?" I yelled. But the geek actually did it; he stuffed the dirt into his mouth with the marshmallows and chewed it all up. Then he spat it out with a huge throw-up sound. Nice.

I just gave up and walked out of there. I didn't have time to yell at Henri anymore. Sally's friends were going to start arriving any minute, so I ran down to the house to get changed. I put on my black turtleneck, the old tuxedo pants of Dad's that Mom made over for me, and the black cape with the red lining that I got for my birthday. And none too soon, either, because a couple of kids came while I was getting dressed, and the rest seemed to arrive all together.

Suddenly there were little kids all over the place. Sally was jumping around like a monkey. I called for Henri, because I wanted him to take the kids up to the barn while Pat and I got the food ready, but of course just when I needed him, he was nowhere to be found.

There were kids everywhere, I don't know how many — Sally invited her whole class, I think. But Mom got them calmed down, and Pat and I got the food together, and Sally led the gang ahead of us up the hill towards the barn.

It was a perfect night. It was getting dark. The sky looked almost purple, with a big jack-o'-lantern moon already up and just a few wispy clouds floating around. The air was cool and crisp, but not freezing, and it smelled of my parents' fire and the two pitchers of cider I was carrying. Up ahead the barn door was wide open. You could see the scarecrow like a black cutout against the light of the open door.

The kids were all dressed up like cowboys and princesses, and they were getting excited. They giggled and fooled around, yelling "Boo!" and pushing into each other like little kids do. One girl was singing

"No-body loves me
Ev'ry-body hates me,
I'm gonna go eat worms!"

Then she'd wriggle her fingers at the kid next to her.

"So far, so good," Pat muttered beside me. She

was carrying a big tray of hot dogs in rolls that smelled great. "I hope we've got enough food, though. There are so many kids. Make sure Henri doesn't eat everything."

I was just about to tell her about Henri eating dirt when the scarecrow gave a kind of lurch away from the barn door, picked up a pitchfork from the ground, and with a huge roar lunged at the first set of kids. The kids screamed bloody murder, and my heart stopped beating. Pat went, "Glargh!" and grabbed my shoulder, and I sloshed cider all over my sneakers. It was just a second before we realized that of course the scarecrow was Henri. He had thrown out the scarecrow's stuffing and put the clothes on himself. I heard Pat swearing under her breath.

We ignored Henri and managed to get the kids inside and quieted down so we could pass around the hot dogs and cider. Of course there was plenty — Mom had planned the amount. But I made Henri wait to eat till we'd passed it all out. Then I watched as he pigged down about six dogs in thirty seconds.

"Pretty funny, eh? I was the scarecrow? Har, har, har."

I didn't say anything, so of course he punched me in the arm. "Just cool it, Henri," I warned him. It was all I could do not to slug him back.

Pat left after supper. For a minute, just a split second, I wanted to ask her to stay. But the kids seemed to be eating happily, so I ducked into one of the cow stalls, where I had stashed my magic gear. Just as I realized my hat was missing, I heard Henri from out front.

"Step right up, laydeez an' gennelmen! Magic show, eh? Step right up for 'Enri 'Oudini, greatest on earth."

I couldn't believe it. He'd started without me. I was so ticked off! He was already waving around my top hat and going into his tricks, which I had planned to put in the middle of my act, just in case he botched them.

He botched them. The handkerchiefs for the Handkerchief Hat are made of thin silk compressed into a little disk. You're supposed to hide the disk in your hand and then smuggle it into the hat, so you can pull out this long stream of handkerchiefs. But when Henri reached into the hat, he pulled the first handkerchief too hard and the whole disk flipped into the audience. The kids pulled out the rest of the hand-kerchiefs, laughing all the time. The Disappearing Wand went even worse. There's nothing to this trick — it's just a collapsible wand — but when Henri tried to palm it and stick it in his pocket after collapsing it into the hat, he dropped it loudly on the floor. A little boy crawled forward fast as a beetle, picked it up, and showed everybody how it worked. The kids were laughing so hard I thought a couple of them were going to puke.

I was boiling by the time I stepped in to take

over. I don't know if it was because I was so mad or what, but my tricks never went smoother. I kept up a lot of fast talk like you're supposed to, and the kids all clapped and shouted. But all the time one small corner of my mind was plotting a way to get back at Henri, first for stealing the show and then for ruining it. Then I thought of a variation on the egg trick I always end my show with. It's not a hard trick, but little kids love it because it makes a mess. The idea is that you hatch a chicken out of an egg right on stage. Real magicians use real live chickens, but I have a wind-up chicken like the kind they sell in parks in the spring. But before you "hatch" the chicken, you crush a few raw eggs and look really amazed and embarrassed that there are no chickens in them, and everybody laughs. Then you crush a plastic one and release the wind-up chicken in a puff of smoke and little colored springs that bounce all over the place. That's the way the trick is supposed to work. But I had an inspiration. I would show that creep Henri he couldn't mess with me.

I stepped forward and announced in a lordly voice: "And now, for my last trick, I need the special magic of Henri Houdini to help me hatch an egg right before your eyes!" Henri wasn't sure what was happening, but he came up to the front, with this grin on his face and drool at the corner of his mouth, looking sideways at the barn walls. I sat him on a little stool in front of my card table, and began.

"Concentrate, Henri Houdini. Concentrate! Bend your magic with mine to hatch this egg. Yes! Yes!" And then I dropped the egg, hard, on the table, and of course it broke all over the place, splashing him.

"Harder! Harder!" I urged Henri, and cracked another egg to his left, closer.

The kids began giggling. Their laughter inspired me and I began throwing eggs at Henri's feet and shoulders and arms, talking louder and faster as the kids began cheering. I took a final egg and crushed it right on top of his head while I released the chicken with an extra dose of smoke bomb.

The kids were clapping and hollering and laughing, and Henri turned and looked at me. It was the first time he had ever looked *at* me, right in my eyes. I could tell he was ripped, but there was another expression, pure black, in those beady eyes of his. Then he looked over my shoulder and gave a smirk. I wondered if I'd gone too far.

Henri got up and sloshed water over his head from the apple-bobbing pan, to clean off the egg, and I took the kids through the Black Widow Spider's Web. That went okay because I could keep an eye on everyone, including Henri, who did nothing worse than make a lot of kids share their candy corn with him. Then I told him to come help me put the blindfolds on for the next part of the House of Horrors.

The idea was to divide the blindfolded kids into

two groups. I'd take the first group through Scream Your Guts Out in the horse stalls. Then Henri would take that group through the Walk to Terror while I finished with the second group, and we'd all meet eventually in the cellar and eat poisoned mushrooms and scream like crazy.

The kids were all milling around blindfolded, playing a sort of blindman's buff, the bigger, feistier kids bumping into the others. Some of them were already yipping about wanting to take their blindfolds off. I quickly sorted out the wimpier ones and took them through the eyeballs and vampire's blood, yelling over my shoulder to Henri to keep an eye on the others till I turned over my group to him. The kids were properly grossed out by the horrors, and I brought them out to Henri to take upstairs, only to see that he'd found a rope somewhere and had tied the bigger ones, boys mostly, neck to neck, like a chain gang. I was really worried that if anybody tripped, they'd choke.

"Stop getting so fancy," I told him. "That could really be dangerous! Now take this group upstairs. Come on, get *going!*"

He grunted and took my group away, and I untied the others and led them to Scream Your Guts Out. I could hear the younger kids climbing the stairs ahead of us, some of them laughing and going "Ick!" and "Yuck!" as their faces or hands hit the sticky flypaper I had hung in the stairwell. Then suddenly

I heard someone scream in real terror, and I flashed out around the horse stall just in time to see Henri with a little girl in each arm pretending he was going to drop them or throw them off the staircase. He shook one, and the other began to slip. I suddenly had a vision of little kids lying on the barn floor like broken dolls.

"Henri! Don't! Stop!" I shouted, and he laughed and shouted something back in French which I couldn't understand but I could guess. But he pulled the girls back into the line and went on up. My heart was pounding. The guy was a maniac!

I went back to my group. A couple had torn off their blindfolds and were tossing the eyeballs into the vampire's blood and at the other kids. They seemed to be enjoying themselves, though, so I just sorted out the mess and kept on with it until I could hear Henri move his group downstairs into the cellar. Then with my group I started up to the hayloft. I was hurrying now, because the kids were getting rambunctious, and I was nervous about what Henri would do next.

I didn't hurry fast enough. We were through the flypaper and across the Pit of Hell when something started to bother me. I told my group to stop and be quiet. I just wanted to listen to what was happening downstairs. I took a deep breath to listen. I couldn't hear anything. Not a single sound coming up from the cellar.

"Come on!" I said. I began grabbing blindfolds and tearing them off. "Hurry up. Follow me."

We clattered downstairs into the cellar, where it was pitch dark. Henri had turned off the light. That was okay, it was supposed to happen, we both had flashlights, and Henri's group was supposed to jump out and scare us, but before I even switched my flashlight on, I knew no one would be there.

Then I heard a high-pitched, frantic screaming. It was coming from outside, some distance away. I wanted to run toward the sound, but I had this bunch of kids; I quickly counted them and made them buddy-up so I wouldn't lose them. Then we went outside, and I could hear the shouts and yelling coming from up near the old water tower. I could see some dim light up there, too, and I thought I heard Sally screaming at the top of her lungs. I tried to hurry, but it was tough going up the hill. Even with the moon and my flashlight, kids kept tripping and stumbling and falling. It was like one of those nightmares where you're running for your life but your legs move like molasses.

I couldn't believe the scene when we got to the top of the hill. Henri had herded his group to a tree near the water tower, and tied them all to it, wrapping the rope around and around. He was dancing up and down in front of them, holding the flashlight beneath his chin and making scary faces.

"Now you will burn!" he was shouting. "Burn at the stake like witches! I will light the fire right now any second!" I saw him go to Sally and take one of her braids in his hand. "I will light this 'air. It will sizzle and smoke and catch like dry grass! You will go up in smoke!"

Sally gave one of those yells that sounds as if it might turn into crying. I saw red. I bolted ahead of my group, ran up and grabbed Henry by the arm, and spun him around.

"What the hell are you *doing*?" I shouted. "Leave her alone!" It felt so good to shout at Henri that I went crazy and attacked him. I just threw myself at him. We went down, and that felt great, too, and I kneed him in the stomach and hit him and hit him in the face until he curled into a ball and put his arm over his head. Then I suddenly heard the kids whooping it up, and I stopped.

"Yay! Yay! Our hee-ro!" Sally was yelling. All the other kids were shouting, too. Henri was crying. He got to his knees, wiping his nose.

"What'd I do wrong?" he blubbered. "I was 'elping. Why do you 'ate me? Everybody does." He got to his feet, shaking his head and snuffling. "It's fun to hate 'Enri, eh?" He stumbled off toward the house, casting a long slope-shouldered shadow ahead of him in the moonlight.

I didn't say anything as I untied the kids from

the tree, but I didn't have to; they were all chattering and laughing. I took them back to the barn for the finale, which was bobbing for apples. Most of them got soaked, and that was it; the party was over. I was never so happy to see a party end.

Back at the house, the kids' parents were waiting outside, and they all drove off, thanking Sally and my parents and me for a great time. And then Uncle Harry and Aunt Michelle and Henri came out. Aunt Michelle came right over to me and lifted her hand. I thought she was going to slap me, but she took my chin and gave me a kiss.

"Thank you so very much," she said, "for including Henri." She pronounced his name "Ohn-ree"; she's the French speaker in the family. "I hope he didn't scare you with the post."

"The post?" I looked over at Henri. His face was even grosser with a swollen lip and dried blood just under the nose.

"Yes, hitting the post while running in your game!" she laughed. "What a silly!" She pronounced it "seely."

I looked over at Henri. Who are you kidding? I wanted to ask him. Why are you covering for me?

"Yes, you scared me," I finally blurted out, trying to catch his eye. He was looking over my shoulder again. He kind of shrugged and headed for their car. I watched him walk over and get in as all the others said good-bye. His head was down. The song was in my head,

> No-body loves me,
> Ev'ry-body hates me,
> I'm gonna go eat worms!

I felt I should have said something to let him know that maybe I'd gone too far when I saw him teasing Sally. Shaken his hand or something, tried to make it up. It was so strange how I could hate him one minute and feel sorry for him the next. When the car went by me, I waved, but he was looking the other way. The car was past me before he stuck a hand out the window.

I was bone tired. I dragged myself back up to the barn to clean up a little and turn out the lights. The place was a mess, and I decided to leave most of it till tomorrow. All I wanted now was to wash the vampire's blood and raw egg off me and go to bed. I went back down to the house, thinking I could just sneak off upstairs, but Mom called out from the kitchen. "Ned, come on in a minute." I walked over and leaned on the sink where she was washing coffee cups.

"Ned, dear, thank you for being so kind to Henri. I know he's not the easiest boy, always trying to attract attention like that. We're proud of the way you managed it."

Proud. Can you believe it? We said goodnight, and I went upstairs. I thought of Henri stuffing that dirt into his mouth with the marshmallows, and the way he kept making the kids scream.

As I passed Sally's room she called out to me. She was lying there with one of her teddy bears, her braids straight out against the pillow.

She popped up into a sitting position. "Ned, the party was *so neat*. Everything was! I bet it was the best Halloween ever. And even old Henri was good, don't you think? I mean, those magic tricks of his? They were *so funny!* And then scaring us in the loft, and tying us to that tree? And then you coming in, and him pretending to let you beat him up and everything! It was perfect!" She laughed. "I guess he's not as bad as we thought," she went on when I didn't say anything. "I mean he's pretty bad and all. But not that bad. He probably can't help it."

I stood there thinking how good it had felt to hit Henri, and how terrible it felt right now.

"Yeah, I guess that's it," I said. "Bad as he is, he probably can't help it." I paused. "Anyway, he's our cousin."

"Yup," she said, snuggling under her covers again. "G'night, bro'." She grinned. "Don't let the geeks getcha."

I laughed. "I'll try not to," I said. I punched her lightly on the shoulder as I turned out the light. "Good night, eh?"

The Thanksgiving Turkey

IF HALLOWEEN WITH Henri was a fight, then what I got into with the Thanksgiving turkey was out-and-out war. It had begun on a day back in June when I got home from baseball practice and found Dad waiting for me outside the house. His face was pink, which meant he was really excited about something.

"You won't believe what I got for you, Ned!" he said. "Come take a look!" He walked over to the station wagon and opened the tailgate door.

In front of me was a large plywood box with a lot of airholes.

"Inside that," he announced proudly, "is a turkey. Bronze-feathered. Purebred. Five months old. Already weighs sixteen, seventeen pounds. By Thanksgiving he'll come in at thirty or thirty-five."

27

"It's . . . for me?" I said. I stared at the box.

"Till death do you part," Dad said with a little laugh. I stared at Dad. "Oh, yes," he said cheerfully, "that's the Thanksgiving bird, all right. He'll feed everybody!" By everybody, he meant the aunts and uncles and cousins from the Scott side of the family who would come for Thanksgiving dinner. It was our turn.

"Hold it. You mean we're going to raise him and kill him right here at the house, is that it?" I said.

"*You're* going to," he corrected.

I didn't say anything; I just stood there.

"Look, Ned," he said, "here we are on a farm." He swept his arm out over our land. It's not really a farm at all. It's a couple of acres, plus the old barn, in a country town near Boston. We never use the barn except for parties like Sally's and when the church borrows it for barn sales. "Here we are on a farm," he said again, "yet you're as ignorant of how food gets on your plate as any city boy. This bird will fix all that."

"But, Dad. Wait. Why me?"

"Ned, we went over this last week. Real life! Hands-on experience!"

Here we go again, I thought. Lately Dad had started to worry about whether he was a good father. "I don't take you fishing," he'd tell me. "I don't take you hunting. Just think of Uncle Jack and Frank, fixing up that old Ford together. Why, I haven't even taught you how to work with wood." He'd sigh. "It's terrible. How can you get tuned for reality if no one teaches you how to change the spark plugs?" Dad's in advertising, and when he gets these terrific enthusiasms he begins to sound like a TV ad. A piece of the Rock! The Pepsi generation! Get tuned for real life!

The thing is, Dad doesn't like fishing or hunting or woodworking himself. But it seemed to make him sad that he couldn't teach me to like them.

I guess that's why he had decided to teach me other things. The trouble was that at first he hit on stuff I knew more about than he did. Like baseball. I had come home from a game last week just as he got back from work, and he started right in. I had gone three-for-four and was feeling pretty good. He saw me with my bat and glove and said, "Say, Ned, let's see that stance of yours." So I dropped the glove and got into my stance with the bat. He shook his head.

"Same one you used last year?"

"Right."

"Bat right beside your shoulder. I notice you don't cock your wrists much."

"Right. Not till the pitch."

"I don't see how you can get any hits at all like that."

"Dad. I'm batting .421."

"Really? How about power?"

"Just a few doubles. One triple. No homers."

"See? Not much power."

"Dad. I'm a lead-off hitter. I'm short and fast; I hit a lot of singles and draw a lot of walks. I get on base almost two out of every three times I come to the plate. What d'you want?"

"It's not what *I* want." He sounded really surprised. "It's what *you* want." He looked at me sort of confused. "Don't you want homers?"

I didn't know what to say to that. I mean, sure, *everybody* wants homers. So I just shrugged, and then he shrugged, and then we went inside.

Now, what the new turkey had to do with all that, I didn't know exactly. But something.

"You'll see," Dad said. "We'll learn a lot from this bird."

"We?" I said, cheering up.

"Well, I mean to the extent that I'll certainly help you build a turkey coop. . . . I think that's what they're called."

He reached into the station wagon and pulled out the big box, and the thing inside immediately began flapping and banging around, rocking the box and making it hard for Dad and me to hear each other. I went over to help him and we sort of staggered with it to the storage shed, which is off the pantry next to the kitchen. The turkey would stay there until we built the coop. I don't know why Dad chose the shed instead of the barn, except that we just weren't used to using the barn for anything, and besides, we'd put our kittens and puppies in the shed when they were getting housebroken.

We set down the box and opened its door. The turkey stopped its cackling and thrashing, and strutted out into the middle off the shed floor. Dad was right: the feathers were bronze. The bird looked big and strong. He had a fat stomach and huge wings and long scaly feet with big toenails that looked like claws. A piece of bright red skin was flipped over his beak, and hung way down. Dad said it was called a wattle. The bird stood there quietly in the middle of the room, moving his neck a little. He looked kind of bored, actually. Dad left to move the car, and I filled a dog bowl with the feed pellets Dad had brought, and another bowl with water. I kept one eye on the turkey. He didn't move much. I closed the door and left.

During the night he crapped all over everything in the shed. Next morning, we built the coop.

Dad didn't know much more about carpentry than how to saw wood and hammer nails: one reason he hadn't taught me to work with wood. But we managed to put up a small, rickety kind of lean-to near the barn. It was made out of some thin lath wood we had lying around, and it had a little entrance door in front, like a doghouse. It took us the longest time to figure out how to build a frame for the thing without any kind of plan to go by. Each of us would hold up three or four pieces of wood to see how they looked, and then they'd all fall down. Mainly we just propped and nailed as we went. With chicken wire and some nice hickory stakes Mom had bought for her tomato plants, we built a small yard for the turkey in front of the coop. Then I went down to the house to get the bird.

Inside the shed I picked my way through the scattered pellets and crap and backed the turkey carefully into a corner. His beady eyes watched me. I moved slowly to the left. He moved slowly to the right. I gave a quick fake to the right, and when he dodged left I dove and got him with one arm. He flapped his free wing like crazy and almost knocked me down, but finally I got both arms around him so he couldn't move his wings.

He turned and bit me in the neck.

People say that turkeys don't bite, they only peck, but people are wrong. This turkey *bit*. It felt like he had *teeth*. He held on tight. I yelled and dropped him, naturally. Then I really went after him. I thought I was small and quick, but compared to that bird I was big and slow. I dove and grabbed for him again, but got only air. I faked right and went left, and he faked left and went right. When I got him in a tight corner, he came at me with the beak, and I had to turn and run. I came back at him with a yell, but he flapped away sideways and I tripped and fell in the pellets and crap. I rolled right over and with a diving tackle got him by his bony legs, yanked him to my chest, and got him in a kind of half nelson so he couldn't bite. I held him that way, and a lot tighter than I had to, all the way up to his coop. I chucked him into the entrance door and gave him a kick to get him all the way inside. I was breathing hard and my arms were shaking, but I tried not to let it show. I nodded to Dad and walked pretty calmly out of the yard, and fixed the chicken-wire fence behind me. There was a short silence.

Then the turkey demolished his coop.

I am not exaggerating. He went berserk and just tore the place to bits. There was some wild screeching, then some flapping and banging sounds, and suddenly some side boards popped out of place, then the roof was knocked off-center, then most of the left side blew out and the turkey roared through the entrance door, knocking it down the way a fullback would bowl over a lousy interior lineman. The whole coop collapsed behind him and he tore off toward the chicken-wire fence and hit it with a full head of steam, his legs still going after the hit. The tomato stakes swayed and then snapped off like trees in a hurricane. The bird got tangled up a bit in the chicken wire, but he freed himself quickly and flapped over to a spot near the barn door, where suddenly he stopped cold and began looking bored and stupid again.

I can tell you, my father and I were awed.

Dad said softly, "I'll be —— !" And he almost

never runs out of words. He looked at the bird, looked at me, and shook his head. His shoulders drooped. I could tell he thought he'd blown the fatherhood thing again. He figured there was no way in the world that he could teach me how to feed and raise and kill that turkey.

So suddenly I just had to do it.

"Don't worry," I said quickly. "I'll figure out a way to manage him."

"Really?" Dad perked up immediately. "Good for you, Ned!" He snapped his fingers. "You know what? Maybe you could keep him in the barn!"

"Why not?" I said brightly. "There's nothing else in there!" Then I heard myself say, "And I'll build a better fence around the barn door. A strong one this time. I'll use those big iron rods down cellar."

"Terrific idea!" he said. "Hard work, but it'll be great for your wrists and forearms. Strengthen 'em. For baseball, I mean."

Well, it just about tore my wrists and forearms *off*, carrying the iron rods up to the barn from the cellar, but at least the work brought me to my senses. I went back down to the house and called Vic Wyluda.

Vic's my best buddy anyway, but I would have called him then even if I hated him. Vic is a grade behind me in school, but he's a head taller and twenty pounds heavier, and if they ever send me off to fight in a real war, I'm not going without Vic. Besides, it so happens that Vic's father builds houses for a living. Victor *knows* stuff.

He came over carrying a sledgehammer and some wire cutters, and in about half an hour we had a really strong fence built in a semicircle around a side door to the barn. Vic had left the sidedoor open, and now he slid the main door open, too. He took a broomstick he found in the barn, and handed me a long piece of lath wood. We found the turkey pecking around in my mother's Concord grapes. We chased it with the sticks all the way through the barn door, and shut it in.

"I'll bet that's the only barn in town," Vic said before he left, "that's used to keep in a single turkey."

"In town?" I said. "In all of New England!"

"In the whole country!"

"In the world! The universe!"

Actually the barn *was* used for one other thing. It was where my older sister, Pat, and her friend Annie smoked cigarettes. Pat had other friends, but Annie lived the closest and smoked the most. Her father was a lung cancer specialist, and he gave lectures in all the schools about smoking and lung cancer. That's why Annie smoked over at our place, never at home. Pat and Annie knew my father would blow his top if he found them smoking in the barn. He had told Pat that if she wanted to ruin her health, she would have to do it outside the barn, because she was sure to light a fire smoking in the barn, and a fire would kill her a lot quicker than cigarettes would. But none of these warnings about fire or lung cancer bothered Pat and Annie. They *liked* smoking in the barn.

I thought they'd get mad when I put the turkey in there, but they didn't. I don't know that they actually liked having him around, but as time went on they sure liked making me nervous when *I* was around.

"What's his name?" Annie asked me one day, taking a deep drag.

"I'm not going to name him anything."

"You're *not*?" she said with a lot of fake surprise on her face. "Why not? He's so *cute*."

"Cute, my eye."

"He's not going to name the turkey," Pat said, "because he's got to kill it in a few months. He's got to chop off its head with an ax, and then its body will run around for a while with no head at all."

"Thanks, Pat," I said.

"Don't mention it. Then he'll hang it up by the feet and let all the blood drain out. And then . . . well *then*, Annie, he'll eviscerate it."

"Eviscerate?" Annie opened her eyes wide. "Gee, what's that, Pat?"

"Eviscerate means he'll cut him open with a big knife and take all the guts out."

"The guts? Oh, *I* get it! You mean the *guts*," Annie said, still playing straight man.

"Right," Pat said. "The gory, gloppy, gishy guts. Then he'll dunk him in boiling water and then pull out the feathers one by one with a pair of pliers. Or does that come before the guts?"

"Wow. He'll sure have to use both hands to get the guts out of such a *big* turkey, won't he?" Annie said, then: "No, don't go, Ned. We like talking to you."

"Yes," Pat said, "we really enjoy talking about your . . . *pet*." Then they both started laughing and cackling like crazed turkeys.

It was really Dad's fault that Pat was being such a jerk. He had brought home instructions on slaughtering the turkey, and he got the brilliant idea of sharing them with the whole family. "Ned has volunteered to do the work," he explained, "but I want all of us to know what it's going to take to do it."

So he started reading through the instructions. "A clean, sharp ax should be used for the beheading," Dad read with great interest. Pat and Mom stared at each other, then Mom looked away. "The swift, hard chop severs the spinal cord at the juncture of neck and body, causing instant death," he continued. Mom began to look a little green. Pat rolled her eyes. I tried to figure out how to hold the turkey and chop off its head at the same time. Finally, Sally said, "Yuk! I'm not going to eat any of *that* bird."

"Then in theory," my father said, "you should eat no turkey at all; don't you see?"

"All right, I won't."

"Ever."

"*Fine* with me." For a little kid, Sally's pretty stubborn.

"The point is," my father said, "that all of us who eat meat have a responsibility to know and accept how it comes to us. The farther we get from that, the farther we get from real life. Not to mention honesty. We have to be honest."

"Right," Pat said. "Brutally honest. Completely, brutally honest. Otherwise, we can't eat meat, right? And I happen to *like* turkey."

So that explains Pat. She was trying to be brutally honest, and she stayed that way week after week, at least about the turkey. The minute I'd appear in the barn, she and Annie would start in on the fine points of slaughtering. Finally I just kept out of there during their smoking sessions.

The thing is, as the weeks went by, the turkey seemed determined to make me *want* to kill him. There were only three things that bird could do, but he did them all really well:

1. Eat
2. Crap
3. Escape

Of course, I didn't mind feeding him or watching him eat; who would? I hadn't expected to have to clean up after him so much, but Dad said turkeys could confuse their food pellets with their own "droppings," so I had to make sure that at least his eating area was clean, and since he scattered his pellets all over the barn, that meant cleaning most of the barn.

But what really got me was the way he kept abusing our fence. Vic and I really had built it strong. The iron rods were so thick and deeply set that a big dog could hit one full tilt and just bounce off. I guess it was the chicken wire. We should have used the kind of chain-link fence they have around schools. But I'm not sure that would have worked, either. That bird was the Houdini of turkeys. I never saw him do it, but I would come home from school, and there would be another hole. The turkey would be strutting around in Mom's Concord grapes on the hill near his yard, and Mom would be mad. He never went very far until I came after him. Then he would take off.

At first I tried to corner and catch him the way I had the first time in the shed. But the longer he lived, the bigger and stronger and faster he got, and the more of a fool he made of me when I went to catch him. Even when I caught him, it was no bargain. I already mentioned his biting, but you didn't want to get near his wings when he was flapping them around, either. Left jab, left hook, right cross, he had it all. He was the Rocky of turkeys.

So I used the broomstick method more and more. I'd get him between me and the barn and walk very casually toward him holding the broomstick. When I got close enough, with a quick flick of the wrists I'd give him one in the tailfeathers. Whap! Buh-GURK! He would leap in the air and flap a little closer to the barn. In this way, I'd sort of herd him toward the big door. But it took me longer and longer as he learned to keep his distance. He had a quick eye and good reflexes. If I did hit him, he would leap in the air and flap to one side *away* from the barn. He was stubborn and mean.

By November, when I came toward him with a broomstick, he would sometimes turn and face me, cocking his head, staring through the long red comb that hung over one eye, his wattle quivering below his neck. The cold, beady eyes would go right through me. I'd back down. It just wasn't worth the fight to get him inside. Besides, he wasn't going anywhere. Why should he? He owned the barn.

But the big day was coming, and I knew it. Though I half wanted the turkey to take his forty or forty-five pounds and just disappear someplace, I also knew that if anything like that happened I'd feel cheated.

No, I had to kill him. I wanted to put him on the table and give thanks. Not for health or happiness or a good batting average, but just for getting him the hell out of my life. I would do it myself, too. Even Vic Wyluda couldn't help me now. Even Dad couldn't, though he tried.

"Look, Ned, you don't have to feel locked into this. I don't want you to feel trapped."

"I'm not trapped. The turkey's trapped."

"I'm serious about this, Ned."

"So am I."

"I'll help you if you want. Your mother thinks I should hire someone else to do the whole thing, and perhaps she's right. She usually is."

"Not this time. This time she's wrong."

He opened his mouth to say something more, and then closed it. He gave me a strange look. At last he said quietly, "You . . . you've read those instructions I brought home?"

"Three times."

"Have you thought about how you're going to proceed, step by step?"

"Lots."

Dad took in a lot of air, then let it out. He looked a little nervous. That was okay with me, because I was, too. "Well," he said, "just try to stay calm. And be sure to call on me if you want help."

I nodded my head. "Sure," I said.

Two days before Thanksgiving, early in the morning before breakfast, I walked up to the barn carrying an ax, a pair of pliers, a large pot, and a long rope. Pat, who was good at knots, had tied a slipknot for me, making a noose at one end of the rope.

"What's this for?" she said as she tied it.

"I'm going to hang the turkey up by the feet in order to . . . you know."

She stared at me for a minute, then looked away. "You're really going through with it, aren't you?"

This made me mad. "Well, what'd you *think* I was going to do after all this? Just let him live?"

She gave me a hard, straight look. "Yes, as a matter of fact," she said. "That's exactly what I thought you'd do. Just let him live."

The look on her face came back to me that morning as I approached the barn and then walked into the turkey yard through the latest big hole in the fence.

I could hear him clucking around in the barn, so I shut the door that let him into the yard, broke up all the remaining lath sticks lying around, and made a fire to boil the big pot on. After he was dead I was supposed to dunk him in boiling water for a while before pulling the feathers out with the pliers. (Pat had been right about that. But it would happen before eviscerating, not after.) When the fire was going good, I took the ax and the rope, opened the barn door again, and went in.

The turkey was pecking around near an old grain bin, probably looking for food. I hadn't fed him any pellets for the past couple of days, because I wanted him to be hungry. I threw one end of the rope up over a beam near a wall. I spread the noose end of the rope open on the floor as far away from the wall as it would go. Then I put some food pellets inside the noose, went and got the other end of the rope in my hands. I waited for the turkey to put his feet in the noose. The idea was that as soon as he did that, I would pull on the rope and he would swish right up into the air, held by the feet.

Looking back, I can see I was crazy to expect this plan to work. I bet I even got the idea from a cartoon or something. It's the kind of stunt Wile E. Coyote would try against the Road Runner.

Except that it worked. Crazy, right? The bird came over — immediately! — and stepped with both feet into the middle of the noose. He didn't even eat any food pellets or anything. He just stood there looking very pleased with himself. He probably thought he was messing up some project of mine.

I yanked hard on my end of the rope, and the noose rose and held, and the turkey swooshed upside down into the air with a great squawking and flapping of wings. I let out a whoop! It worked! I couldn't believe it!

I had pounded a spike in the wall to tie my end of the rope to. I tried to tie a half-hitch, but it came undone and the turkey fell to the floor with a loud thump and more squawking and flapping. I felt bad. I got the end of the rope back and pulled him up against the wall again and tied the rope to the spike with a lot of granny knots. My arms were shaking by now. *Most* of me was shaking because of the effort I

was making, and all the squawking and flapping —
and what I had to do next.

I found the ax on the floor behind me and picked
it up. I walked over to the wall and the turkey. He
wasn't squawking as much but he was still flapping
a lot, moving back and forth against the wall. It was
going to be hard to swing the ax just right so it would
cut his head off, but I spit in my hands and rubbed
them together and grabbed the ax handle tight, just
like a baseball bat. I got into a kind of power stance,
my left side facing the turkey, my hands held back
and up, with the wrists cocked. Then I gritted my
teeth, stepped forward, and swung.

I missed him completely.

I must have closed my eyes, or he flapped up-
ward at the last second. The ax head buried itself in
the wall, and the turkey, still hanging upside down,
landed square on my head as I leaned forward. He
had worked one of his feet free from the noose, and
he scratched me with it on the forehead as I pulled
the ax from the wall.

Now he was flapping in circles, still hanging upside down against the wall, and screaming. I started
swearing at him and shouting. I raised the ax again
with shaking arms and swung weakly. I mostly missed
him again, but I must have nicked him slightly on the
wing or leg, because he started bleeding. When he
flapped his wings he scattered drops of blood all over
me and the ax and everything.

I started to cry; I was so mad and scared. He was moving crazily all over the place now, banging up against the wall. I could barely see him through the tears and sweat and blood. I lifted the ax high and swung for the third time, but the ax handle slipped from my hands in the middle of my swing. The ax bounced off the wall and almost got me coming back.

I went crazy. I picked up the ax and choked way up on the handle. I stepped forward, and with a short sure punching swing I cut cleanly through the rope that was holding the turkey up in the air. He fell to the floor with a great shrieking crash and scrabbled across to the door and out into his yard, where he got to his feet and ran like a bat out of hell right through the hole in the fence, making a beeline for the Concord grapes, the long rope trailing on the ground behind him.

I grabbed the ax by the bottom of the handle and scaled it with all my might across the barn. It rose, spinning, and buried itself, thunk! in a beam way up in the hayloft. Then I walked out of the barn and down to the house. I was really confused, and there was no place else to go.

They were all sitting at the breakfast table when I walked into the kitchen. They had been sitting together there the whole time, waiting for me to get it over with.

"Ned, my dear!" Mom said, rising when she saw me. My shirt and hands and forehead were splattered with blood and I was still crying. She probably thought the turkey had slaughtered *me*.

"I cut the rope! I cut the rope!" I shouted fast, so she wouldn't worry.

"What? You what? What did he say?"

"I threw the ax!" I told my father.

"You cut it? Did you kill it?" Sally said.

"The rope?"

"No, the turkey!"

"You *threw* the ax?" my father said.

"Yes!"

"Yes, you killed him?" Sally said.

"No!"

"Ned, you mean the turkey's still alive?" Pat asked.

"Yes!"

"Oh, thank God!" she said, and actually put her face in her hands. I guess she and Annie had really gotten to like that bird, smoking cigarettes up there with him.

"Dad, I couldn't do it," I said. "He was too quick, or my wrists weren't strong enough, I didn't cock them enough, he kept moving, I don't know, I just couldn't do it."

Suddenly Sally began to cry. My mother sat down and put an arm around her. Pat took her face from her hands and began to laugh. My father came over and put an arm around me and said it was all right. Then I was laughing and crying, too. It was pretty complicated there for a while, but finally we all got settled down, and I was sent upstairs to change my shirt and wash up.

From my window I could see the turkey pecking around as usual in the grapes. Later, my mother got into the car and went downtown by herself and bought a big supermarket turkey, which she kept in its brown paper bag and shoved in the refrigerator out in the shed, and Dad went up to the barn to put out the fire I'd lit.

No one mentioned the big death scene again, not even Pat. But I want to tell you what happened two days later at Thanksgiving. Grandmother Scott was there, and Aunt Lise and Uncle Matt came with their kids, and Uncle Fred and Aunt Agnes with theirs, and our second cousins from someplace near Worcester. We were all dressed up, and there was the usual talking and laughing, and a bunch of us played football in our best clothes.

The important thing happened at dinner. Dad brought in the big turkey and everybody oohed and ahhed, and said it smelled delicious, and Dad and Uncle Matt carved it up and served everybody. I was talking to my cousin Jason when someone put a plate in front of me. I looked down at it. There were two big pieces of turkey meat, one white, one dark. I looked at the meat for a long while, and the longer I looked, the more I knew I wouldn't be able to eat it. Maybe tomorrow I would, or the next day, or next Thanksgiving. But not then.

I felt embarrassed. I looked up catty-corner across the table at Pat. She was sitting holding her knife and fork and staring down at *her* plate — just staring. She glanced up and caught me looking at her, and she gave me a weak smile and shrugged. Then the two of us naturally looked all the way down the table to where Sally was sitting.

Sally was having a good time. Her body was moving jerkily, the way it does when she kicks her legs back and forth beneath her chair. She had covered her turkey meat with cranberry sauce, and now she was spooning creamed onions on top of that. Finally she shoved the whole mess to one side and started to eat her mashed potatoes.

Outside I could hear the turkey, our turkey, gabbling and clucking around in the front yard. He had come down earlier from the barn — chest out, strutting with a slight limp, his wattle wigwagging, his beady eyes bright with life. It came to me that one of these days pretty soon we were going to have to give him a name.

The Christmas
Secret

THANKSGIVING WITH DAD's relatives was hardly over before plans for Christmas with Mom's family began to heat up.

My cousin Frank phoned me about a week before Christmas. "You're all coming to Grandpa's next Saturday, right?" he said. "Okay. I'm going to let you in on a little family secret."

"You mean some special present?" I asked.

"Come on, Ned. Would I call you about a dumb Christmas present? This is *serious*, buddy. It involves Grandpa and my father and your father and all the men who'll be there."

"Okay," I said. "Shoot."

"I'll shoot you, all right," he warned, "if you tell anyone about this."

"Frank, buddy, how can I tell anybody anything? I don't *know* anything yet."

"You know there's a secret," he said. "That's enough. You go and blab that to your sisters or someone, and we'll have the whole house down on us."

The whole house this Christmas meant just about everyone on Mom's side of the family. Six uncles and aunts and about ten cousins, plus my own family, were all going to Grandpa and Grandma Walker's house. Mom said everybody was going for Christmas this year especially to be with Grandpa while the strike was on. That was no secret to anyone.

My parents seemed pretty worried about the strike. All I knew was Grandpa and his sons, my mother's three brothers, ran a mill, and the workers there had stopped working. They wanted to be paid more money, and Grandpa said there was no more money to pay. Pat said that if the workers got mad enough, there would be a lot of fights and stuff. I had heard Mom and Dad talking about Grandpa's blood pressure, but Dad seemed more worried about what my uncles were going to do.

"Then the secret must be about the strike, right?" I said to Frank.

"Well, let's put it this way. The strike is probably the reason for it. But only part of it. I'm talking about something bigger than the strike, Ned." Frank made his voice very serious. "Much bigger. It's about the whole family."

I was impressed. Family is probably the main reason Frank treats me like a friend. If we weren't cousins, Frank probably wouldn't even give me the time of day. He's only two grades ahead of me, but he's a lot older in some ways. He already knows that he wants to be on the Board of the mill like his father; and he says that after he makes a lot of money he's going to run for governor of Massachusetts, or maybe senator. He's always getting elected class president. He does everything right: hunt, fish, play hockey, sail, tie knots. He's tall, dark, and handsome, and girls call him on the phone all the time.

"Tell you what," he said, "I'll reveal the actual secret to you when we get to Grandpa's. You can look forward to it all week, but you won't be under any pressure to blab and so forth. Okay?"

"Gee, Frank," I said, "how can I thank you for your trust?"

"Hey, Ned, you know what I mean. Right? Okay, see you there." He hung up.

For the next few days, I tried not to think about Frank's secret. Finally the day before Christmas, we drove to my grandparents' for their annual eggnog party. Secret or no secret, I was happy just to be there. Christmas at my grandparents' is pretty amazing. They have a huge house anyway, but at Christmas the place seems like a palace. They always have an enormous tree covered with lights and ornaments in the sunken living room, and a smaller one in the entrance hall with the big fireplace. They have candles and holly and mistletoe everywhere, and lights covering the lilac bushes all down the length of the driveway.

When we got there in the afternoon, the party had already started. The driveway was lined with cars, and people were walking through new snow to the house, waving and calling to each other, their words making puffs of smoke in the air.

"I wonder if Frank's already here," I said, opening the car door before the car had even stopped. It was all I could do not to run up ahead of the others to the house.

Inside the front door, the entrance hall was so packed with people I almost had to push to get in. The air was full of laughter and talking and Christmas music, and it smelled of eggnog and cigarette smoke and perfume and cake. A fat man with a potbelly bumped into me as he called "Merry Christmas" to my mother, and my Aunt Sylvia came over and spilled some eggnog on me as she kissed me off-center on the eye. Sally slipped her hand into mine; she probably thought she was going to be trampled to death. But then Grandma Walker suddenly appeared, and she went right to Sally and gave her a big hug. Sally almost disappeared, Grandma was so big.

"Child?" Grandma said. She has a nice voice, clear as a bell but kind of softened by her southern accent. "Child, aren't you going to take off that *coat*?" When she kissed me, I asked her where Frank was.

"Frank? Why gracious, honey, I haven't seen him. You look for him, he'll turn up. But you say hi to your other cousins, too, now. And say Merry Christmas to your grandfather first, hear?"

I slipped away as she turned toward Pat and my parents, and I stood still for a minute getting my bearings and deciding where to look first. I settled on the living room, but before I could move I felt a hand on my shoulder. It was Pat.

"Ned, could you come over here for a minute?"

"I have to find Frank."

"Yes, but come over here first. It will only take a second." She kept a firm hand on my arm and more or less pulled me into the dining room nearby, where all the food and eggnog was. "See that man over there?" She pointed to a big guy in a white jacket near a large crystal bowl of eggnog. He was ladling the eggnog into cups. "Just go over to his table and get two cups for me," Pat said. "Please? Women aren't supposed to do it, especially at Christmas, and anyway I'm too shy."

"Oh, all right," I said, and went over and brought back two full cups.

"Why two?" I asked.

"One's for you," she said, taking the other. "Cheers." She clinked our cups together. She took a small sip and I took a big gulp of the rich creamy eggnog. I almost gagged.

"Pat, this has whiskey in it!"

"Shh! Jerk. Of course it does. Actually, it's brandy and a little rum, I think."

I took another sip, just to see what it was like. It was really strong. "Where's *our* eggnog?" I said.

"Over there," she answered, pointing to another table with a smaller bowl.

"I guess you think you're pretty smart," I said, taking another swig. "I should have known, you telling me you were shy."

"Yeth, I am," she said. "I'm vewwy, vewwy thy."

"Next thing, you'll be getting me to sneak one of Grandpa's cigars."

"I prefer cigarettes. Besides," she added, looking over the crowded dining room and hall, "Grandpa's got enough problems. Look at all these people, all talking about the strike."

"You think so? At Christmas?" I took another sip of the eggnog. There wasn't much left, so I drank it down.

"Geez, Ned," Pat said, "you'll get bombed if you drink that way."

"Not me." I put the cup down on a nearby table and wiped my mouth with the back of my hand. "Good stuff," I said. Pat laughed, and took a little sip from her cup. We stood there for a couple of minutes. She took another little sip.

"Here," I said. "Allow me to show you a magic trick." I took her cup out of her hands. "Behold." I held the cup at arm's length in front of me, then quickly brought it to my mouth and drank down half. "Abra-cadabra!" Then I drank down the rest. "Gone!" I said. "Incredible, huh?"

"Very funny," Pat said. She gave me a mean little smile. "You're going to regret this, Ned."

"Nonsense, my dear," I said. "And now, if you'll excuse me, I must depart. Your company is fabulous, but I've got to go find Frank."

"Why don't you just do that," she said. She took back her cup. "And Ned?" Another mean little smile. "Please try not to trip over anything."

"Fear not," I said, raising a hand in farewell as I turned and left. The truth is, I did feel a little funny as I walked back through the hall, then through the study. I don't mean that I felt bad, actually. As a matter of fact, I felt pretty good. My body was a little out of whack in a nice sort of way; I felt like I was walking on cushions. The eggnog was warm all through me.

I went down into the sunken living room, where there was another crowd of people. The Christmas tree at one end looked beautiful, and there were greens and big red flowers everywhere. I began circling the big room to look for Frank. It was hard to find a single person in such a crowd. I jumped once to see over someone's shoulder, thinking I had spotted Frank across the room. It wasn't Frank, but jumping helped with the view, and besides it suddenly felt good to jump. I started jumping every few steps as I walked. Then I felt a large hand on my arm.

"Did you think," my grandfather said, "that this was an athletic event?"

"Oh, Merry Christmas, Grandpa," I said. "I was just looking for you." This wasn't true, obviously, and I don't even know why I said it. I thought Grandpa was really a great guy, and besides I was named Edward after him, so I usually had no trouble telling him the truth about anything.

"Looking for me?" he said. "Were you really? Seldom if ever have I seen anyone so eager to greet me."

"Well, I was looking for Frank, too," I admitted.

"Ah. Frank. Well, keep searching. There are a lot of people here." He looked over the crowd with satisfaction. "A lot of people." Then to my surprise he sort of hunched over near me. "They come for a better view of the battle. They smell blood. It won't be mine, though." He straightened up again. The only thing I could smell on him was pipe smoke and the brandy or whatever from the eggnog. "Well, carry on," he said. "Preferably not like a kangaroo."

"Yes, sir," I said. He patted my shoulder and moved off. On my way out of the living room I got stuck in a kind of human traffic jam and had to stand still for a minute or two, listening. Pat was right. A lot of the grown-ups were talking about the strike. It was Edward this, and the Board that, and Jack and his brothers and the vote. I knew *who* they were talking about, but not what. Edward was my grandfather, and Uncle Jack, Frank's father, was one of my uncles. What I didn't understand was why the Board and the vote was such a big deal to all these people at Grandma's Christmas party. I mean, I didn't really expect them to talk about peace on earth and goodwill toward men, but why was the strike so important to anyone but Grandpa? I wondered if Frank knew what it was all about.

I retraced my steps through the study and back through the hall, and headed for the main staircase. Maybe Frank was up in the third-floor dormitory room where a lot of us kids would spend the night. On my way to the stairs I passed a tray with cups full of eggnog. I took one. I figured Frank would like it, and I didn't have to tell him it was Pat's idea.

Up in the dorm room there were plenty of beds but still no Frank. Where was he? I sat down gloomily on one of the beds, and slowly drank his eggnog. They'd have to come *sometime* soon, because the afternoon was passing, and I could see from the window that some of the guests were already leaving the party.

I figured I might as well wait for Frank outside, since there was nothing else to do, so when my cup was empty I got up and walked downstairs again.

The brandy hadn't tasted so strong this time, but I felt sort of dizzy instead of just lightheaded like before, and my legs were heavy instead of springy.

Downstairs the crowd had thinned out a lot, so I went quickly through all the rooms again, just in case Frank had come while I was upstairs. But no. So I put on my coat and went outside. On my way I snagged another cup of eggnog. I wanted to get back the good feeling I had had after the first cup.

I sat on a rock behind a bare bush covered with Christmas lights. I watched people leave, and I drank. It was dusk. The lights on the bushes had been turned on, and through them I could see the red taillights of the cars winking into the distance. Unless I closed one eye, each taillight looked like two or three of them. Also, I was getting very cold. The eggnog wasn't warming me up like before at all. By the time some headlights finally came up the drive, I felt frozen to my rock. I got stiffly to my feet as the car stopped. Its door opened; I heard the voice of Aunt Joan, Frank's mother, and I headed for the house, staggering a little. I didn't want Frank to know I had been waiting for him.

Inside, the warm air with its sweet smells of Christmas made my head spin. I felt dizzy and a little stupid. In fact I didn't feel too good at all. I decided to wait for a while in Grandpa's study. I managed to walk there in a straight line by going very slowly and keeping my legs stiff, as if I had no knees. Maybe I'd had too much eggnog to drink. Luckily, the study was empty, and I plumped down in a big deep leather chair.

From out in the hall, I could hear Grandma welcoming Uncle Jack and Aunt Joan and Frank to her house. Then there was some low talking, and then I heard her say, "I think he's in the study."

A minute later, Frank breezed into the room.

"Sorry I'm late," he said. "Flat tire in Milford. Tough luck, but what can you do? They say there's about an hour before dinner, and we've got a lot to accomplish. You ready?" He sounded terrifically businesslike, as if he was carrying a briefcase or something.

I said, "Huh?"

"What we've got to do first," he said, "is find a route from our bedroom — the dorm room, right? — down to Grandpa's poolroom in the basement. But it's got to be a back route, down the backstairs and corridors, maybe through the cellar. I've thought about this a lot, and even made a plan of the house, and I'm pretty sure we can do it."

I didn't understand any of this. I said, "Frang? Wha's the secreh?" My tongue didn't seem to want to say what I wanted to say. I tried again, speaking very clearly. "What's. The. Secret. Frank?"

He gave me a look, but he was too busy with his

plan to notice anything wrong. "The secret is kind of complicated," he said. "I'll tell you about it as soon as I can, but time is precious now. We've got to get going, Ned. Are you with me or not?"

All of a sudden a bolt of energy shot through me, and I felt wonderful again. "You better believe I'm ready!" I said. I bounced up from the chair. "Remember the Alamo!"

"Shh, quiet!" he said. He led me up to the dorm room on the third floor. We had to put on ties and jackets for dinner, he said, so we might as well get changed now, and then explore. I changed in a jiffy, throwing my clothes all over the place, but I had trouble tying my tie, and Frank caught up with me there.

"Stop acting like a jerk," Frank said grouchily, and then he led me to a small door at the back of the room that I had never noticed before. He opened it, stuck in his head, said "Yes!" and entered, flicking on a light. We were in a big attic storeroom. Frank closed the door behind us and walked across the storeroom till he found a flight of stairs leading down. We took them and they landed us in a hallway, with three or four closed doors off of it, that I had never been in before.

"Maids' rooms," Frank whispered. "Here's hoping they're downstairs." He began quietly to open and close the doors. Bedroom, bedroom, bathroom . . .

"This is *neat!*" I said, much louder than I meant to.

"Shut *up!*" Frank hissed, then opened the last door. "Ah. Beautiful," he said softly. It was another flight of stairs.

"Where do they go?" I whispered.

"Someplace near the kitchen, I think." He was right. The stairs landed us just at the entrance to the kitchen, at the end of a hall by the back door.

The kitchen was full of clatter and mess, because they were cleaning up from the eggnog party as well as getting dinner. There were extra helpers in for the party, but I recognized a tall, thin maid named Karen and a short, fat cook, Bridget.

I could see Frank putting on a big smile as he walked right in. "Hello, Karen. Hello, Bridget. Merry Christmas." He was acting very grown-up. "Can you tell me please where the door to the cellar is?"

Bridget frowned at him. "What do you want down cellar in those good clothes?" she said. She could be a little touchy when she was trying to get a meal on the table.

"Don't worry, we're not going to *play* down there," Frank said as if he was explaining something to a child. "Bridget, where's the door?"

"Ah, you devil! Right over there by the pans closet. Now get out of my kitchen. Go!"

"Hey hey *hey!*" I said brightly for no particular reason. Karen crossed her arms and gave me a steady look. Frank pulled me toward the door. "Remember the Alamo!" I said recklessly as we started down. The two women stared after us.

"What the hell's *wrong* with you?" Frank asked at the bottom of the stairs. But he wasn't the kind of guy who really expects you to answer a question like that, and he immediately turned to cross the cellar floor.

The cellar was big, dark, dirty, and full of cobwebs. It was lit by two light bulbs hanging far apart. In the middle was the old coal furnace they don't use anymore, and beyond it a big pile of leftover coal next to the wall. "Perfect!" Frank said. "You know what's beyond that wall? The poolroom!" He gave me a sly smile. "And the secret."

"Frank, I don't get it," I said.

"You will."

"When? Like, when are you going to tell me, buddy?"

He stopped smiling. "When I get good and ready, buddy," he said. "Right now, you don't seem in the mood to keep secrets." He walked away from me and I followed at a distance, trying to think of a comeback. None came, and I followed him in silence up to Christmas Eve dinner.

The dinner took forever. Everybody at the table — there must have been twenty of us — had the Christmas spirit except me. I hardly said anything to Uncle

Jack, Frank's father, who was sitting right beside me. I felt sad and stupid, and I had a headache. I didn't feel like eating, but there was nothing else to do, so I ate till I began to feel a little queasy. By dessert, which I skipped, my stomach had settled down, but my mind hadn't.

Then Karen came into the dining room with a flaming plum pudding, and after setting it down, she whispered something to Grandpa Walker. "I'll see them in the living room," he said, and rose from the table. The conversation died down as he left the room. "From the union," Uncle Jack said. "The strike committee strikes again." Grandma said, "My gracious, can't we have a Christmas dinner without this?" and Uncle Jack said, "Not if we want to have another one, Mother." Some people chuckled and some people frowned, and Frank caught my eye and winked. When I saw him excuse himself after dessert, I did likewise and made a beeline for him.

"Frank? Come outside for a minute. Okay?"

He shrugged. "Why not?" And once outside he took a deep breath of the chilly air. "Ah, me," he said. "Nice evening for a stroll." He started off down the drive, which was bright with Christmas lights, and I ran and caught up with him, spinning him around by one arm.

"Frank! Will you just tell me the lousy secret and get it *over* with?"

His face was a blank. "Sure," he said smoothly. "On Christmas Eve, Grandpa Walker and the other men in the family go down and pretend to fix the furnace but really they just drink bourbon and hold a secret meeting and discuss all the family business that's important to all of us, okay?" He turned and walked on.

"Wait. What? *Wait,*" I said, catching up. "I don't get it."

He stopped. He turned, raising his eyebrows. He coolly adjusted my necktie and brushed something off the shoulder of my jacket. "Really, Ned," he said. "If you're not going to listen, I don't see much point in telling you anything at all." He walked on.

"I'm listening, I'm listening," I said, frantically catching up to him again. He was smiling now.

"Okay, then," he said. "Listen up. One Christmas a long time ago, there was a big blizzard, and my father and Grandpa were the only men in the house. After dinner the furnace broke down. So they took some tools and a bottle of Virginia Gentleman — that's bourbon. And they fixed the furnace, and drank, and talked a lot. And I guess Grandpa really liked that, and it became a kind of tradition. Just as everybody's getting ready to stuff the stockings for the kids, Grandpa announces about the furnace being broken, and the men take off their jackets and make a big production out of it and everything. And they go down to the poolroom with the bourbon and have this secret meeting. I can't believe I didn't even know about it till this year."

He stopped talking. "Wow!" I said appreciatively. "So go on!"

He gave me a look. "What do you mean, go on? That's it, Ned. That's all of it."

"But I mean . . . Well, what do they talk about?"

"Exactly!" he said. "What do they talk about? Ned, do you have any idea, the amount of stuff they don't tell us? Or even lie to us about? We're never let in on any of the important things. Like the strike, for instance. I heard my Dad telling Mom that the strike would make him and his brothers really face up to it this year."

"Face up to what?"

"That's just it," said Frank. "What has anybody told us about the strike, Ned? *Nothing,* that's what."

This was true, though on the other hand I hadn't asked anybody much, either. Anyway, something else was bothering me. "What I don't understand," I said, "is what all of this has to do with running up- and downstairs to the cellar. All that stuff we did this afternoon."

Frank stopped and turned to me, his face a strange mask in the lights from the bushes. He said, "Ned. Aren't you being just a little thick?"

"Yeah, he's thick!" came a voice. "He's almost as thick as you are, jerk!" We looked up. We had got almost to the end of the driveway. Right in front of us, beside the last and brightest bush, were four boys just about our age. Two of them were already packing snow into iceballs.

"What a cute little tie you got on," said one. "Can I have the next dance?"

"You're on private property," Frank said. His voice shook a little.

"Yeah, we're on private property. What're you gonna do about it? What's old man Walker gonna do about the committee in his house right now, huh? He send you guys down here maybe with a Christmas present?"

"No," said the first. "He sent them down to spy." He stepped forward, packing his iceball. "That's it. To spy on us. Huh? Jerk?"

He kept coming. Frank looked at me. "Run!" he said, and we turned and were gone. An iceball whistled past my head.

"Spies! You tell the old man we *eat* spies down here!"

And that was the moment, running behind him back up the hill, that I finally understood Frank's secret, and what he wanted: for me to go that night with him down the backstairs, past the maids' rooms and past the kitchen, into the dark, cobwebby cellar, and across to the wall of the poolroom. For us to spy on our own fathers at their secret meeting. The thought really scared the hell out of me. Any fog left in my brain from the eggnog suddenly vanished. I bolted past Frank into the lead, running with a head clear as icewater until the big dark house loomed up in front of us.

Much later that night, Frank shook me awake. "Time to go, buddy," he whispered. "Come on."

I sat up. My head went *slush;* it felt like my brain was made of oatmeal. It took me a minute to remember where I was. The room was dark. The others were all asleep. I looked at my watch: 11:25.

"We're right on schedule," he whispered. "Follow me."

I tossed off the covers. I was still wearing my pants and shirt. I put on my sneakers and followed Frank on tiptoe across the dark room full of sleeping kids and into the attic storeroom, where he closed the door and snapped on a flashlight. "I thought of everything," he said. I rubbed my eyes. I had a headache.

We crossed the attic floor, then crept down the first flight of stairs to the corridor outside the maids' rooms. Down that hallway over squeaking floorboards. I was shivering with cold, and with fear, and now my brain felt like an icicle had been stabbed through it. Then we went down the second flight of stairs to the hall outside the kitchen. Frank breathed a sigh of relief and began laughing softly. "That was the worst part," he said. I realized with amazement that he was actually enjoying himself. "You ready?" he asked.

"No," I said.

"Ned, relax. No one can hear us now. Hey, you know what you need? Get you going? A little blood sugar. Candy."

"*Candy?*"

"Trust me, buddy." Before I could argue he pulled me across the kitchen and through the pantry into the darkened dining room. I could hear women's voices and laughter coming from the very next room, the entrance hall with the big fireplace, where they were stuffing Christmas stockings.

"You want to take a peek?" Frank whispered.

"No, Frank, come on!" I started to leave.

"Wait." He drew me over to the sideboard, where there were silver bowls of Christmas candy: chocolates, candy canes, gumdrops, ribbon candy, wrapped caramels. He made me hold out both hands, and he loaded them up. "I've got to carry the flashlight," he whispered, and was gone through the swinging door just as Aunt Sylvia, sounding really close, said, "Oh, I *hope* not, Joan!" In panic, my hands full of the candy, I awkwardly shoved through the door, praying that I wouldn't get caught.

And then I was following Frank down the back cellar stairs, straining in the dark because I couldn't use my hands. It was pitch black at the bottom of the stairs. Across the cellar, light came from two small windows high on the door to the poolroom. Frank shined the flashlight into my face, making me squint.

"We're almost there, now. Whatever you do, don't trip over anything." Then he was gone, and I followed blindly after him, feeling my way with my feet, shuffling, clutching the candy in my hands. The new furnace roared hot air at me as I passed it.

My arms were trembling when I caught up to Frank next to the big coal pile near the poolroom door. I took a breath and tried to wipe my sweaty face with my shoulder. That's when I heard the men's voices through the wall. I had been hearing them all along as a low hum, and hadn't realized it. I stood still.

". . . not so much to ask." The hum was separating into words, spoken by voices I could recognize. That was Uncle Jack. "And not much for you to give, especially on Christmas Eve," he said.

"Not much? I disagree." That was Grandpa. "Christmas feelings have no place in this, though that's what they're counting on. No, gentlemen, we're engaged in a staring contest, and I refuse to blink."

"Isn't it possible," Uncle Jack said, "that you've been staring so long you've stopped seeing what's in front of your eyes?"

It must have been the strike they were talking about.

"I am not blind, Jack. For forty years I have seen where I'm going and what directions to take. And now you tell me my vision is failing."

"Father, we only . . ."

"But you do. The old man's going blind. Poor

old bat. Well, I can tell you I see that I'm in a fight. I just didn't expect to be in it alone." Grandpa wasn't shouting really, but he sounded good and mad.

The other men all began to talk at once. I glanced quickly at Frank. In the dim light from the door windows, his face looked worried. He looked to one side, quickly ran the flashlight beam over the coal pile, and then slowly, carefully, began to climb it. It took me a minute to see that he was trying to get high enough to look through the little door windows down into the next room.

". . . no need to be so defensive," Uncle Jack was saying. "We're in it with you, but you're not listening to what we say."

"Ah! Deaf as well as blind! Well, I grant you, my ears do close when my own sons talk like economics professors about a mill which is my life. My *life!*"

"And a good life, too. But that won't stop the business from disappearing under your nose if you don't accept . . ."

"Can't *smell*, now. *Or* hear, *or* see! What a ridiculous old man I must be, deaf, dumb, and blind, by God!"

I could hear the other men trying to calm Grandpa down. Then Uncle Jack's voice came out ahead again.

"Father, listen! There's something you've got to know. It looks like I'm the one who's got to tell you."

In the sudden quiet that followed, a lump of coal

rolled down from the pile, sounding like an avalanche.

"Father, you know you've lost control of the Board. What I have to say is that if you force this to a vote, we'll vote you down."

I looked up at Frank. I didn't understand what was happening in there. Was it something you could see?

"Frank," I said, "I'm coming up."

"No!" he hissed. "There's no room."

"I've got to see," I said. I dumped the candy on the floor.

Frank pushed the palm of his hand out at me. "You. Stay. Put." It was like I was a pet dog, and a pretty stupid one at that. Something in me snapped. I'd had too much of Frank bossing me around and keeping things from me and making a fool of me with his candy and being better than me all the time. So I walked right up the coal pile without stopping. My momentum almost carried me over the top, and I had to grab him to stop myself. He grabbed me back to keep his balance, and then I lost mine, and the whole coal pile moved, moved like a wave beneath us, and we slid forward in a great rumbling rush of coal and crashed loudly into the poolroom door.

A second of dust and silence, then chairs scraped and voices barked, and the door was flung open from inside. Grandpa stuck his head in. His face looked fierce. Then it began to look just confused. I wiped some coal dust out of my eyes and looked up at him.

"Ah, Ned, I believe. Still looking for Frank?" He almost smiled. "Otis, Jack," he said over his shoulder to our fathers. "It looks like my own sons aren't the only source of surprise around here. Sons in general are a surprise, it seems."

"Ned," said Dad, appearing at the door beside Grandpa. He pulled me up into the poolroom. "Frank. Are you two all right?" We mumbled that we were. Dad said, "In God's name, what were you doing?"

I said, "We wanted to sort of listen in on your meeting." I was embarrassed. "I guess we wanted to be in on the secret."

"What secret?" said Grandpa.

"I don't know; I didn't understand much."

Grandpa smiled. "One seldom does understand much," he said, but he seemed to be talking to the men, not to us. "Sometimes you just have to hope that you will, eventually. Given time. When you're old enough, like me."

"Let's go on upstairs now, you two," Uncle Jack said. "We'll talk about your prank tomorrow."

"We will do no such thing," Grandpa said fiercely. "Tomorrow is Christmas Day." His voice softened. "Tomorrow we celebrate the birth of the Son. You should rejoice in your sons on such a day. As I rejoice in mine. Come on, boys," he said to us. "Back where you came from. High time for bed." He put a hand on each of our shoulders and walked us out of the poolroom into the cellar. At the door he turned back towards the men.

"It's been a long day," he said. "You all go on fixing the furnace. I'm off to bed. I'll not force a vote. Consider it my Christmas gift. I accept your plan."

I didn't know exactly what had happened, or what to say. I waited for Frank to say something, but for once he was quiet.

"Grandpa," I started, as we walked across the cellar.

"Yes, Ned."

"I'm sorry we interrupted."

"It's just as well you did, Ned. It's time for me to step aside and follow my sons. It's just not easy; that's all. Sometimes it takes a youngster to remind us that blood is thicker than pride."

"Thicker than water, you mean," said Frank.

"No. I meant what I said."

We walked up the backstairs to the third-floor bathroom. Grandpa stood at the door and watched us sponge off the coal dust. I would have liked to hear what Frank thought of all this, but with Grandpa there I couldn't ask. Just before we went in to bed, Grandpa said, "What you boys stumbled onto was no secret. Just a family quarrel. And the family's stronger than the quarrel. There's nothing for you to worry about. I meant what I said about rejoicing. That's what Christmas is for. Goodnight, now."

We slid quietly into the dorm room and got into bed. It seemed I could hear Grandpa's footsteps going down and down for a long time.

It took me a while to get to sleep. Grandpa had said there was nothing for us to worry about, but that didn't feel like the whole truth. I knew he'd meant all of it, though, when he said that Christmas was for rejoicing. So finally that's what I kept in my mind until there was nothing there at all except for Frank's quiet breathing in the bed near mine, and farther away my sisters and cousins, all together there in the one big room in my grandfather's house.

The Valentine Daze

JANUARY WAS GRAY and depressing, especially when my summer girlfriend, Marcia, wrote late in the month that I shouldn't come visit her, like I'd planned. Total bummer. But I didn't do anything about it until I saw all the red hearts and streamers go up in the window of Lane's Pharmacy. That's when I decided I wouldn't take no for an answer.

I walked right in and bought a Valentine's card. It was kind of corny, but it would do. It had a picture of a cupid knocking on a door. The cupid had little wings and was holding a bow and arrow. Beside the cupid, it said:

KNOCK KNOCK!
WHO'S THERE?

LOVE!
LOVE WHO?

Then, when you opened the card, it said: LOVE, ME! In the space under LOVE, ME!, I wrote:

Dear Marcia:

> *I'm going to knock on your door on Valentine's Day in the afternoon. No matter what you say. No kidding. Enough with these letters! My buddy Vic will drive me to the bus station in his T-Bird. What a guy! The Memory of Your Kisses!*
>
> *Ned*

I read the letter over and counted up the words: forty-five. All of Marcia's letters were fifty words or less. She said that the best love letters, in her opinion, were no more than fifty words long, since "a lover's heart fills with love, not words" (that's from her very first letter). Marcia's letters were more poetic than mine, but at least I never went over the fifty words. It wasn't easy, either, because you had to allow for the last sentence, which had to be one of these three:

> *"Tonight my thoughts are full of love, and you."*
> *"You are blossoming in my mind like a flower."*
> *"The Memory of Your Kisses!"*

This was Marcia's idea, too. The letters were almost like a puzzle or game to her, and she liked making up rules. It was a pain at times, but basically it didn't bother me. After all, Marcia was the one with the experience.

In this particular letter I had enough room for "Tonight my thoughts are full of love, and you," but lately I was pretty much sticking to "The Memory of Your Kisses!" because, to tell the truth, the memory was getting a little dim. I hadn't kissed Marcia in six months. I hadn't *seen* Marcia in six months.

I also might as well admit that my buddy Vic Wyluda doesn't have a license, much less a Thunderbird. My father was going to drive me to the bus station. But Marcia's parents were so terrible — really cruel when they were home, she said, but they went out to parties most nights — that I didn't like reminding her of my own parents, who weren't bad. Besides, Marcia had these older boyfriends, named Mike and Curt, who had motorcycles. She said they were ex-boyfriends now that I had come into her life, but after six months I had to wonder, even though she kept telling me not to. Just last week she had written a letter about Curt.

Dear Ned:

Forget about Curt. Curt and his Honda are dead in my mind. Killed by your first kiss. Your arms and the moonlight. He won't roar back into my life. You alone are there with the stars, the lapping waves, the moon. You are blossoming in my mind like a flower.

Marcia

The stars and the waves and the moon were all part of the first kiss, which of course is important because without it there wouldn't have been any Valentine's Day visit, or even any letters. No one would believe how it really happened, but that's okay — neither do I, and I was there.

The scene: A yacht — a forty-foot ketch, to be exact. Anchored in a little cove on the coast of Maine. There are only four or five other boats around. It is late at night. There are stars and a moon and lapping waves, just like Marcia told about in her letter. The owner of the boat, Mr. Fitzpatrick, is ashore with some friends from the other boats. That leaves my cousin Frank and me on board. Frank had been asked by Mr. Fitzpatrick to crew for him on a Labor Day weekend cruise, and I was invited to come along. With Frank and me are two girls — Valerie, whose father owns one of the other boats, and Valerie's friend, Marcia. Frank and Valerie are way up front in the bow of the boat, and Marcia and I are back in the stern. We are dancing to music from a radio. The music is slow and we are dancing really close, and I can't believe what's happening, because Marcia's sixteen, and I only met her about an hour ago.

This is typical of Frank, of the way he works. I

mean, Mr. Fitzpatrick goes ashore in the boat's only dinghy — it's just about dusk now — and pretty soon Frank spots these two girls over in another boat pretty far away. We've been watching these girls through binoculars all day while we sailed. Frank waves to them and they wave back. Then he goes down into the cabin and returns with some signal flags that neither of us knows how to use, and he waves them all over the place making fake signals, and we can see the girls laughing. Then he makes a big deal of pointing to the ship-to-shore radio, and he turns it on, and pretty soon is talking and laughing with the girls, and in another two minutes he's talked them into rowing over to us in their boat's extra dinghy, even though it's almost dark by now. While they're on their way, he runs around not even talking to me, getting out the pretzels, "borrowing" a couple of beers, getting the right music on the radio, and so on. Then when the girls come on board, he does almost all the talking. He shuts off all the lights except the running lights so we can watch the moon come up, and he sits real close to Valerie. Pretty soon he gives me a wink, and suddenly he and Valerie are walking hand in hand up toward the bow, and there I am, alone with this other girl, trying to stay cool.

She's really pretty, especially her eyes, which are green and wide apart. She's only a little taller than I am. She has a way of looking at you, level and steady and knowing everything about you. She sits there looking at me that way, her face lighted by the moon, and stars all around her head, and it's all I can do not to jump overboard, though I hang in there the best I can.

"It's really a beautiful night, isn't it?" she says.

"Yeah. Boy. Terrific."

"The stars are so bright and clear in a harbor like this. It's one of the best things about cruising, don't you think?"

"I'll say. *The* best, probably."

"It's like, life is so complicated on shore, and so simple on the sea."

"No kidding. I mean absolutely, yes."

We go on like that for a while, and then I ask her to dance, or she asks me, I don't really remember, but suddenly there we are, dancing to this slow music, closer and closer. Just as I'm wondering if I dare kiss her, she draws back a little and gives me that look again, and I sort of fall forward and we're kissing.

This is definitely not the kind of thing that happens to me much ever. And then later, when the girls are getting ready to leave (because they think they hear Valerie's father and his friends on shore getting ready to come back to the boats), and Valerie is actually stepping down into the rowboat, Marcia pulls me aside and puts her arms around my neck and kisses me again quickly and says, "I'll tell you tomorrow what I think. It always takes a day to sink in, but I do believe I'm in love with you." And me thinking that if love means wanting to look into someone's eyes for about a hundred years, then in my case I don't even need a day to think about it.

We spend most of the next day sailing back towards Marblehead, where we started from (and where Valerie and Marcia live), and that night, our last night together, we have to spend at a big cookout ashore with everyone who's been sailing together. But Marcia and I sit mostly away from the others and talk. That's when I learn about Mike and Curt and their motorcycles. And how Marcia's mother wants her to be a model and keeps pushing fancy clothes at her, but Marcia just knows she's going to be a poet and has already written lots of stuff.

Toward the end of the cookout, the moon comes up again over the water. It's very romantic. Marcia looks up at it for a long time, and I can tell she's getting ready to say something special. Finally she says, "Why? . . . Why?"

"Why, uh . . . why what?" I say, not sounding too cool.

"Why should anyone," she says dreamily, "fall in love with someone who lives so far away?"

"You mean . . . me?" I'm not exactly covering myself with glory here, I know, but luckily it doesn't seem to matter to Marcia.

"Yes, I mean you," she says. She stops looking

at the moon and turns her eyes on me. The moonlight is on her face again, and her eyes go right through to somewhere in the middle of my stomach.

"I don't live that far away," I say. "I'll come visit you."

"Ned." She shakes her head. "You don't know. My parents. I don't even want to talk about it."

"Then you can come to my house. Or we can meet in Boston or someplace. There's got to be a way."

"Yes." She smiles up at the night sky. "Love will find a way." She turns her eyes on me again. "But listen, will you do something for me?"

"Yes. Anything." I really mean this. I want her to ask me to climb to the top of that pine tree over there and jump off, or maybe swim out to the boat and fetch her sweater and keep it dry all the way back.

"Write," she says.

"Write? You mean poems, like you?"

"Letters. Every week. *To* me."

"Oh, *letters*. Sure! Of course I will. Letters, yes!"

"But really? Will you write what's in your heart? Promise?"

"Yes. I promise."

"Every single week?"

"Yes. Yes, I will."

Anyway, that's how the letter-writing got going. At first I was all set to write one every day, but when I got home I realized I didn't know anything about writing love letters, so I was really relieved and happy when I got her first one just a couple of days later.

> *Dear Ned,*
>
> *How can love be kept alive? A thought a day. A letter a week. Your picture on my mirror. (Send one!) Memory. Nothing can destroy what we have — not Mike, not my parents, though they try. What keeps me strong? What makes my heart sing? The Memory of Your Kisses!*
>
> > *Marcia*
>
> *P.S. In my opinion, love letters should be short but full of love. After all, a lover's heart fills with love, not words. I believe we can pour our feelings into 50 words or less. Go ahead, count the words in my letter.*

Well, there are fifty words on the nose — not counting the P.S., of course.

The funny thing is that the letters worked. At least I thought about Marcia a lot. I wasn't really good at writing, not like Marcia, and I spent more time trying to write fifty words or less than I would have just blabbing along the way you usually do in a letter. We sent each other pictures, and I had to spend a lot of time on that, too, trying to get one that looked okay.

But I learned a lot about Marcia as the weeks went by. I learned a lot especially about her parents. In one letter she said they were "unbearable, abominable, and abrasive," and I had to look up *abominable* and *abrasive*. They had to be very rich, because her mother kept buying her all these clothes to make her into a fancy New York model, and her father kept changing the sports car he kept for his private use; at first he had a Jaguar, then he swapped that for a Maserati, then a Corvette. Also in one letter she said, "Curt keeps calling, a bee after honey. But he knows better than to drive a motorcycle around *this* neighborhood. The poor fool." Then sometimes she'd just write about how much she wanted to hold me close and kiss me on the couch in their living room, but her parents would kill us both. I had these dreams of driving up to her house on my motorcycle and just taking her away.

It was hard, though, to keep her real in my mind on fifty words a week. I mean, the fifty words a week were real, all right. And I had photographs of her and could picture her in my head when I tried hard. But it was harder and harder to get back the feelings I'd had on the boat or at the cookout all those weeks and months ago. So in January, two or three weeks after Christmas, I cooked up a plan, called the Greyhound station in Boston, and put it all in a letter.

Dear Marcia,

Love will find a way! How about this for a great Valentine's present: Me! (?) Only $10.50

*by bus. I can come see you. Or you could come
to Boston. We can go for lunch and a Celtics game.
They're really awesome! Tonight my thoughts are
full of love, and you.*

Ned

Fifty words on the nose without even trying, and
I thought that must be a good sign. That shows what
terrible instincts I've got, because her answer came
in less than a week.

Dear Ned,

*No! It cannot be! My parents freak out at
the mere mention. Summer will come with its kiss
of sun, its touch of moon, before I hold you in my
arms again. You are far, but our love is strong.
Still you are blossoming in my mind like a flower.*

Marcia

This was getting to be too much. I know that all
parents do crazy things from time to time, and some
parents are really awful to their kids. But what kind
of parents would say okay to a cruise with a bunch
of kids they don't know, and then freak out when
their daughter wants to see a friend at home? I was
stumped, so I didn't write any letters at all for a couple
of weeks. But Marcia did. Her letters had a lot in them
about kissing and stuff. Finally, I said the hell with
it; I'm going to go see her no matter what her parents

do. That's when I wrote the letter about Vic and his T-Bird and coming to see her no matter what. I waited to mail it until I knew she wouldn't even have time to write back. Then on Valentine's Day, which was a Saturday, my father drove me into Boston, and I got a bus for Marblehead.

In order to arrange all this, I had to tell my parents a couple of small lies, and I got Pat to tell a big one about Marcia's mother calling and inviting me for the afternoon. (My parents get a little uptight about invitations, too.) But it worked out fine, because my Dad had work to do in Boston that day, so he could pick me up at the bus station again in the late afternoon.

I got out at Marblehead and asked directions at a drugstore to 42 Rockland Street (Marcia's address). The girl behind the counter told me it was about a mile out of town. I chose some chocolates from behind the glass case, and the girl put them in a valentine-shaped box. "That for your girlfriend?" she said, winking at me, and I grinned back as I fumbled for the last of my money.

I began walking. To tell the truth, I had never taken a trip like this on my own before, and I was really happy the way things were going so well. It was a sunny day, cold but not freezing, and it felt good walking along past a lot of beautiful houses, mansions some of them, wondering what Marcia's would look like.

I found Rockland Street and turned down it. Did I have the right address? I mean, the houses on Rockland Street were nice and everything, but they all looked pretty much alike, about medium sized, and close together. They looked just like normal houses. I went back to double-check the street sign, then I walked up to number 42 and knocked on the door.

There was a pause of just a few seconds, and then the door opened wide, and there was Marcia.

She was standing just above me, so the first thing I noticed was her clothes: jeans and a green sweatshirt. For some stupid reason, I guess I half expected her to be wearing the kind of model's clothes her mother was always buying for her. Then my eyes went up to her face. Her hair was a little longer than before, and curled up at the edges, but basically she looked the same. Basically she looked great.

Then she took a step toward me and swung the door half shut behind her, and she said, "I *told* you not to come. You're going to ruin everything. Why did you have to do this?"

"Well, I . . . Look, don't worry," I said, though of course I didn't really know what her parents would do when they found me there. But I had come this far, and there was no point in turning coward now. "Can I come in?" I said. I felt stupid just standing there. Somehow I had missed the right moment to give her the box of chocolates.

The door behind her swung open then, and a woman stepped up beside Marcia. She wasn't fat — just plump, I guess you'd say. She was wearing old jeans and a man's blue workshirt, and she was holding a sponge. She had a nice face, and her hair was pulled back and held by a bandanna.

"Heavens, Marcia, why are you keeping this person out on the stoop?" she said.

"This is Ned," Marcia said, as if that explained it.

"Ned Scott," I said, trying to be sort of formal.

"Why, Ned, how nice to see you. Marcia's talked about you." She smiled and put out her hand to shake. "Excuse the grime. Please come in. I'm Marcia's Mom."

We shook hands, and she stepped back. Marcia turned and walked away without a word, so I went inside.

"Here, let me take your jacket," Marcia's mother said as Marcia disappeared into the living room. "Can I get you some cocoa?"

"Well, okay. Thanks," I said, just as Marcia loudly said, "Not right now!" from the living room. Her mother smiled at me, hung up my coat on a hook near the front door, and left. I found I was still holding the box of chocolates, and I took them with me into the living room. Marcia was sitting on the edge of a chair next to a couch. She was sitting turned away from me and her back was very straight. I walked

around the couch and sat down in it. I put the chocolates on the coffee table. Marcia looked over at me
and gave me that level, steady look of hers that I
remembered. She looked like a queen in her jeans
and sweatshirt. She didn't say anything.

"Marcia, what's going on?" I asked.

She didn't move a muscle. "What's going on,"
she said, "is you've decided to stop trusting me."

"What do you mean? Of course I trust you!"

"I told you not to come. I told you why."

"But Marcia . . ." I took a quick look over my
shoulder at the doors of the room. "Your mother is
like . . . *normal*. I mean, I'm almost completely pos-
itive she's not going to attack me or anything, you
know?"

"I see. So now you know everything about my
mother."

"I'm not saying that. I'm only saying . . ." And
just then her mother came into the room carrying a
cup of hot cocoa.

"Left over from breakfast," she said cheerfully,
"but drinkable. You sure you don't want any, dear?"
she said to Marcia.

"I'm sure."

Her mother smiled as she handed me the cup.
"I don't know whether Marcia's got no sweet tooth
or just incredible self-control for a fourteen-year-old,"
she said to me. "Ah, well. I have enough sweet tooth

for both of us. I'll be in the kitchen if anybody needs me." She smiled again and left.

I looked over at Marcia. "Fourteen?" I said.

"Yeah. So?"

"You told me you were sixteen."

"Did I? I guess I must have *felt* sixteen, then."

"I mean, talk about trust."

"Well, after all, I'm taller than you, anyway," she said. She hadn't moved at all in her chair. She didn't look embarrassed or confused or anything; she just sat there with her straight back, looking at me. Part of me was thinking, Boy, this kid's really a *liar*, and another part of me was thinking she was even prettier and older-looking than I remembered.

There was a clatter of feet on the stairs and a man bounced into the room. Her father, I knew it right away, the way you do sometimes. He had the same wide-apart eyes as Marcia. He was wiry and balding, and he was wearing a winter parka and jeans. It was definitely a jeans type of family.

"Marcia, honey," he said, "I'm going to the hardware store. Where are those books you wanted me to drop off?"

"In a bag by the front door," Marcia said without turning.

"Okay. Hiya," he said to me with a wave as he left the room. "How're ya doin'?"

"Fine," I said to his back.

"Good grief," he said from the hallway, then

stuck his head around the doorway. "Don't you ever read anything but romances? Rot your mind. See you later." He grinned at us and disappeared.

I got up from my chair and walked to a window that looked out on the street. The garage door was open, and pretty soon I saw Marcia's father drive out and turn onto the street in his car. It was a Volkswagen Rabbit.

I turned back into the room. "Nice car," I said.

She got up from her chair. It was the first time she had moved at all, and she moved fast. She came right over to where I was standing by the window, and she said, "You don't know anything! You're so smart, aren't you? Well, what do you know, smart guy? Huh?"

"Hey, come on, I didn't say anything," I said. "I just don't think your father's going to kill me, unless he went to the hardware store to get an ax or something."

"Ha ha, very funny. Smart guy, funny guy. What do you know about my parents or my life or *anything*?"

"Look, you were the one who said your parents were so awful. Rich and awful. Unbearable, abominable, and abrasive. See? I remember."

"Well, maybe they are."

"But you made your mother sound like a witch, and I thought maybe your father beat you or something. When he wasn't buying sports cars."

She just stood there looking at me, narrowing her eyes. Then she said, "Maybe he does. Maybe he . . . maybe he *pushes* me." She gave my shoulder a little shove. "Like that." She gave me a stronger push. "Like that!" A hard shove. "That! That! That!" She wasn't taller than me anymore. I had noticed that standing by the window, but it didn't matter, she was so mad she was pushing me all over the room.

"Marcia, cut it out!" I said, trying to keep my balance, and that's when I backed into the coffee table and knocked it over and fell down, and the chocolates went all over the floor. "*Now* look what you've done!" Marcia said, and she jumped on top of me and began punching me in the stomach. "You're so smart you're *dumb!*" she yelled, and pulled my hair. Then I got mad and put her in a headlock, but I couldn't tie her arms up and she kept yanking my hair, so I turned her over and tried to pin her. To my surprise, she flipped *me* over and started pummeling me again, but I caught one of her arms, rolled her off me, and tried to jump on top of her. She was quick and strong. We went rolling around the floor until suddenly she began to giggle and say "The chocolates! The chocolates!" because we were smushing them all underneath us. I began laughing, too, especially when she started tickling me, and finally we just stopped.

We were sitting there on the floor, panting and red in the face. Marcia peeled an orange cream off the rug and popped it in her mouth and said, "So how's school?"

So we talked about each other's schools, and some of our friends. I told her about Sally, who's a violinist in a special youth orchestra, and how Pat had just decided to quit smoking, and Marcia talked about how lonely it felt sometimes to have no sisters or brothers at all. We crawled around the floor as we talked, peeling the mashed chocolates off the rug and eating them. We put the undamaged ones back in the box for later, but then we ate those, too.

After all the chocolates were gone there was a silence for a few seconds while I tried to figure out how to ask her what I wanted to ask her. Finally I just said straight out: "Marcia, how come you made up all that stuff?"

She looked down and picked at the rug a little. "Well," she said, "I guess I thought it would be fun. I thought it would be more interesting. You know?"

"Well, maybe, yes," I said. "But I mean, why would you say all those things about your parents? They don't seem like monsters to me. They're just ordinary."

She looked up. "Right," she said. "Just ordinary. We're very ordinary. We live in an ordinary house and lead ordinary lives and do ordinary things every day, day after day after day."

"You mean you get bored."

She sighed. "I mean I feel like I can't even breathe sometimes. Like I'm in a cage. Don't you ever get that way?"

I thought about it. "I guess I do. Yes. But then something usually comes along to change it. Or I go out and play ball or something, I don't know."

"Well, I make up stories," she said. "I always have. Usually I just write them down for myself. I want to be a great writer some day. But this time I wrote them to you." She gave me a look that was almost shy. "I admit it did get a little out of hand, though. Once I got going, I didn't quite know how to make it stop." She smiled. "But you did. Boy, did you ever. Thud."

We both laughed. It was almost time for me to go if I wasn't going to miss my bus, and we hadn't said anything about whether we were ever going to see each other again. It seemed strange not to mention it at all, so I said, "Where are you going to be this summer?"

"Right here," she said, "unless Valerie invites me to go to China or someplace on her father's boat, which I doubt, because we had a sort of fight last week. Mainly, I'll be around here baby-sitting. What about you?"

"I'm not sure. We usually visit my grandmother on the Cape for a couple of weeks. Mostly I'll be around home, though, mowing lawns and stuff. I've got summer baseball."

We looked at each other. "Well, maybe . . . ,"
she said, her voice trailing off.

"Yeah, maybe we can meet someplace," I said.
We both laughed, a little embarrassed.

"I guess I better go," I finally said.

"I guess so," Marcia said.

We went out into the hallway, and I got on my
jacket. Marcia went and stood at the bottom of the
stairway that led upstairs from the hall. She put a
hand over her heart and stretched her other arm out
towards me. "Adieu, my love," she said. "Adieu,
adieu, until we meet again."

I laughed and stretched out my own arm. "Yes!"
I said. "Till the moon rises and the hoot-owl returns,
and all that stuff!"

She lowered her arm and there was a little pause,
and then she stopped smiling and said, "I want you
to know that I really liked getting your letters."

"You did?"

"I really did. They were so . . . Well, I just loved
them."

"Yours were good, too," I said. "In fact, they
were pretty amazing. I bet you really will be a great
writer some day. I'm sure of it."

"Maybe I will, then," she said. She walked up
to me and put her arms around me, and hugged me.
I hugged her back tight.

"Good-bye," she whispered in my ear. "Good-
bye."

"Good-bye, Valentine," I said.

It was colder on the way back into town, but I hardly felt it. I was thinking about when I first met Marcia, and then all those letters, and what had happened today. It felt strange to be leaving her now. She really was blossoming in my mind like a flower.

The Passover
Easter

I'D BEEN LIVING for Easter vacation all through March. Easter vacation began the Saturday before Palm Sunday. By Palm Sunday morning, I wished I was back in school.

What happened was that at church that morning I got roped into acting in an Easter play. There would be rehearsals every day of vacation. We got a new assistant minister a while ago who's hot on youth groups, and Mom made a deal with me that if I'd join up with Mr. Hurd's group this spring, I wouldn't have to go to all the regular Sunday services. It had seemed like an okay idea at the time, but no one mentioned a dumb play.

On top of that, Grandmother Scott had come down to stay with us for Easter week as usual. When she's around, it's hard to act natural. She's old, she's never casual, she has a big nose like a witch, and she's always talking like she expects to hear something back from you. But I can never tell what that something is. I get riled, Pat gets more smart-aleck than ever, and Mom gets nervous about what we might say. Only Dad and Sally act normal. This particular morning Sally was full of herself because she'd been invited to a seder dinner to celebrate Passover with her friend Debbie Epstein.

Sunday lunch was a disaster. I was in such a rotten mood because of the play that I was hardly even hungry. But it was Dad who really ruined my appetite.

We had just sat down at the table except for Sally, who Mom had already called twice to stop practicing her violin. I didn't blame Sally for not hustling to the table. Who'd want to eat that dinner? It was a huge plate of asparagus with hollandaise sauce, and baked potatoes and salad. Mom doesn't let us eat any meat the week before Easter, to celebrate Lent. When we complain she tells us that people used to fast and give things up for the forty whole days before Easter, so a week is the least we can offer to remember Christ's death. What could we say to that?

Anyway, Dad was sitting there with the salad bowl in his hands, and he said, "I've just had the most tremendous brainstorm."

"Everybody duck," Pat said.

"Pat. Please," Mom said.

"One of my favorite words," Grandmother Scott said. "Brainstorm. A storm in the mind."

"So what it is, Dad?" I asked.

"It involves you, actually," he said.

Sally came bouncing into the room, playing an imaginary violin and whistling. "Did I tell you," she said, "that the Epsteins are having quartets after the seder, and I'll get to play?"

"How marvelous!" Grandmother Scott said. "Now come sit down. You're late to Sunday dinner." She patted the empty seat next to her, and Sally skipped over and gave her a big kiss and sat down. Certain musical prodigies can get away with anything. if Grandmother Scott is around.

"This is the first asparagus of the season, Mother Scott," Mom said.

"Perfectly delicious," Grandmother said.

Sally picked up her asparagus and was eating it like a sword swallower. "Sally, use your fork," Mom said.

"It probably tastes better that way," Grandmother said.

"Grandmother, did you know that I get to drink four glasses of wine at the seder?" Sally said.

"Wait a minute," I complained. "Nobody's giving Dad a chance to tell his brainstorm."

"Which happens to involve you," Pat said.

"Right."

"Otis?" Mom said. "Do you think you could pass the salad bowl while you talk?"

Dad passed the bowl and cleared his throat. "Well," he said, "I'm going to Florida tomorrow. That's not the brainstorm, of course. You know about that already. The brainstorm is that I take Ned with me."

"Oh, Otis dear, no," Mom said.

"Why not? Pat came with me to New York last year. It's Ned's turn. Sally next. Surely Ned's not too young to swim in a motel pool while I work?"

"It's not that, no. But . . ."

"Just listen. The Amplex offices are in Tampa. Tampa is less than fifty miles from Winter Haven. Ned and I could catch the Red Sox's last exhibition game before they come north for the spring. If I can finish up at Amplex in time, we could have a day at Disney World, which is just down the road, and still be back here Thursday after a swim in St. Petersburg."

"Oh, *wow!*" I said.

"Otis, Ned can't go," Mom said. "The play."

"The play?" Dad said.

"I can get out of the play," I said quickly.

"What play?" Dad said.

"Dear, you weren't paying attention. It was just this morning. Ned agreed to be in Mr. Hurd's Easter play."

"Oh, my Lord," Dad said.

"I tell you I'll get out of it. I'll call somebody."

"Ned, you've made a commitment and you've already had a rehearsal . . ."

". . . Just a read-through . . ."

". . . and even if you hadn't, I doubt very much if you could just call somebody up and get a good replacement. I happen to know that Mr. Hurd was already desperate to find someone to play that crippled boy."

"A crippled boy?" Pat said. "You're going to play a crippled boy?"

"Just a minute," Dad said.

"You've got to be kidding," Pat said.

"Pat, hush," Dad said. "Ned, I apologize to you. I really am very sorry. But no, your mother is right. Mr. Hurd and Reverend Mr. Barstow have tried so hard to get a youth group going. I can't cause you to let them down. And the very next business trip I take to a place you want to visit, you'll come with me no matter where it is and even if I have to take you out of school. All right? That's an ironclad promise."

I looked down at my plate and shrugged.

"A crippled boy?" Pat said again.

"Ned, this play sounds interesting," Grandmother Scott said. "Tell me about it." I felt like swearing, and I would have, too, if Grandmother hadn't been there. Instead, I had to tell her about the play.

"Well, this crippled kid's name is Cedric. He spends the whole play in a wheelchair. I guess he's given up on life, 'cause he's in a rotten mood all the time. But then a little girl he knows gives him a butterfly cocoon to watch over. He keeps it beside his chair, see, and somehow he gets interested in watching it." I wasn't looking at Pat, but I could just *feel* her look down at her plate in order not to laugh. "So at Eastertime, the cocoon hatches out into a butterfly and flies out the window. Cedric suddenly understands a lot of stuff he didn't before, and starts to live again. That's the end of the play."

As Cedric, I was basically supposed to spend the whole play being nasty to everyone and dumping on my parents when they tell me how beautiful life can be. *"On Wings of Joy* is the title," I said. One endless act, I thought.

After I told the basic plot, there was a little silence. Then Grandmother said, "Yes. Chrysalis into butterfly. A powerful symbol of rebirth in all religions."

Then there was another silence. Then Sally said, "I guess it's kinda corny, huh?"

That's the way Sally always says things like that, a bullseye out of the blue. Then she added, "Do you want to know something funny about Mr. Hurd? A lot of the kids call him Mr. *Nerd*." She giggled, like that was really scandalous or something.

"Is that what you think is funny, Sally?" I said. "You know what I think is funny? I think it's funny the way you talk all the time about the wonderful

Epsteins, so we can all understand how great the famous cellist for the Boston Symphony Orchestra is, and of course his beautiful wife, Wimphead, or whatever her name is, who writes all those books, not to mention their handsome son Saul, youngest boy ever to play at Wimbledon, and oh I've forgotten little Debbie, who's probably a movie star and I don't even know about it yet. That's what I think is funny."

Sally just sat there looking at me with her big eyes, as the laughter disappeared from her face. Her jaw began to tremble and I saw her clamp her teeth tight to stop it.

"Ned, that was completely uncalled for," Mom said. "If you can't be good company, you might as well leave the table." I got up and stomped out of the room.

So that was Palm Sunday, and the week went downhill from there.

Every morning we had a rehearsal. With only a week to get this skit together, you'd think everyone would be serious, but no. The two kids who were my mother and father in the play — Gail Schmidt, who's in my class at school, and Vic Wyluda, who's usually my best friend — loved hacking around and asking for breaks and playing tricks on Mr. Hurd. And yes, everyone does call him Mr. Nerd behind his back. He's this really skinny guy with a wispy mustache Vic swears is a fake, and wrinkles across his forehead. He speaks just about every sentence like it was a question, and says things like "Let's take our places, please?" "Let's pull ourselves up by our bootstraps, please?" "Let's *lend* ourselves to the author, please?" He waves his arms around a lot, and his shirttails are always coming untucked.

Then there was Genevieve Larkin, playing the girl who gives Cedric the cocoon. Genevieve is a year ahead of Sally at school, and she's the kind of girl who always wears fluffy dresses, the kind of girl Mr. Hurd would always ask to pass out the play booklets. Well, after a couple of days, Genevieve started following me around everywhere and asking my opinion about everything, giving me big smiles and looking at me with these great cow eyes. Of course, Gail and Vic loved this. Gail would get behind Genevieve when she was talking to me, and put her hand to her heart and blow kisses; and Vic would take me aside in a so-called fatherly way and, imitating Mr. Nerd, say things like "Son, let's not take advantage of that lovely young girl? Let's keep our intentions honorable, son?" As for me, I had no trouble at all playing a kid who's in a lousy mood all the time.

After rehearsal I'd just go home alone, since Vic was working for his father on a house. The afternoons were even worse than the mornings, because Grandmother Scott had got it into her head to teach us kids all about spring wildflowers. We took nature walks, if you can believe it, every afternoon rain or shine, and it was mostly rain. Pat got out of it, because she had a job all week at the supermarket to earn money for a car she was going to buy as soon as she got her license. So Grandmother would tell Sally and me to put on our boots, and off we'd go through the melting snow and mud patches, across the field towards the woods in back of our house. Grandmother wore Mom's old down jacket and a plaid wool scarf tied over her bushy gray hair. She walked like a witch, sort of bent over my grandfather's old walking stick that has a silver duck's head for a handle. I think walking was hard for her, but she kept right at it. Sally loved it, skipping around in the field water, whistling her music, practicing her fingering in the air. And Grandmother would talk and talk, trying to teach us stuff.

"Easter and Passover are both religious events, of course," she'd say, "but they are also celebrations of the land's renewal, the firstfruits of the earth. Move those old leaves a bit, Sally, and you might see something." And Sally would move the leaves, and sure enough find a little purple or white flower. "Hepatica," Grandmother would say, or bloodroot, or snowdrop, or whatever it was. And she'd look at me with a smile and I'd nod, thinking about Dad in the hot Florida sun watching a ball game.

Dinners were the worst of all, because Mom had gotten really interested in the seder dinner Sally was going to. Mom is interested in all customs that have to do with food, and it turned out that the seder is full of that kind of thing. So Sally got a chance to

show off even more than usual. We had already heard
about how Passover is about the Jews' escape from
slavery in Egypt, and about how God passed over
their houses on his way to kill the Egyptians' first-
born, and all that. Now we heard about the special
foods that get served at the seder to remind everybody
of that time. Like, there's lamb to remind everyone
of the lambs the Jews sacrificed the night before they
left Egypt, marking their doors with the blood, so the
Angel of Death would pass over.

Right in the middle of dinner you'd hear Sally
say something like "The Jewish people mix apples,
nuts, spices, and wine to recall the bricks which the
Israelites were forced to make without straw." Sally
had been reading books so she could answer Mom's
questions, and Sally is someone who can remember
a thing almost exactly the way it appears in the book.
You can guess what kind of grades she gets in school.

I was getting pretty fed up with all of this, and
postcards from Dad just reminded me how sick I felt
of the rest of the family. "I've discovered a little-known
fact about the seder," I said once after Sally had been
sounding off. "After dinner everyone has to eat two
spoonfuls of dirt to remind them of the sand that got
into their picnics in the desert." And Sally said, "I
bet you're just being mean 'cause Genevieve is madly
in love with you and she's driving you crazy."

I didn't say anything then, but it made me mad
that she even knew about it. I went up to her room

after dinner and interrupted her practicing (Sally actually likes practicing and can do it all day and all night).

"What was that crack about Genevieve? What do you know about her?" I said.

"Nothing," she said, but she looked nervous.

"Sally, if you don't tell me, I'm going to break your violin in two and slash up all of your stuffed animals."

"All right, all right, it was just a joke," she said. She moved so that her bed was between us. "I saw her downtown on Monday, and she was asking what you thought of her, so I said you thought she was the best actor in the play and that she was really beautiful and you wished she was old enough to ask for a date and . . ." She was already backing out of the room and I was after her, and when she got outside she began yelling, "Mom! Help! Ned's hitting me!" Which I wasn't, yet.

That's the way it went all week long. When I wasn't hating rehearsals, I was being bored on nature walks or fighting with Sally or telling Mom there was nothing to do and hearing her say that I could clean the living room or dining room or help Sally dye eggs. A lot of relatives were coming for Easter Sunday lunch, and there was plenty of work to do, but I wasn't going to dye any eggs with Sally this year. Finally Dad got home from Florida and said he didn't have much fun, but I pried out of him that he really did go to a Red

Sox game, and they beat the Tigers 8-6 and there were four home runs.

It was the worst vacation ever.

Dress rehearsal was Saturday afternoon after a whole morning of regular rehearsal. Mrs. Wyluda came to the community center to help us get ready. Genevieve was supposed to wear her hair in pigtails with ribbons and a fancy party dress, and she asked me three times if she looked all right. Mrs. Wyluda had brought along his father's vest for Vic and a ragged old shawl for Gail; they looked exactly like kids playing dress-up. I was supposed to wear a bathrobe and sit in my wheelchair with a blanket over my knees. We all had to put on makeup, which the girls liked. I even had to wear lipstick and rouge, because I was supposed to look flushed like I had a fever. It made me feel like a jerk.

"Remember the season, boys and girls?" Mr. Hurd told us before we started. "Jesus died on the cross and was reborn to eternal life? Cedric, too, is reborn from a death of the spirit, shall we say? That's the splendid moment we have been working toward all week. Let's see it happen, now? Hallelujah!" He raised his arms just like a symphony conductor. "Hallelujah!" That's the kind of pep talk Mr. Nerd had been giving us for the past five days. Vic could do what was probably a very funny imitation of Mr. Nerd with a Polish accent, but I couldn't even laugh.

The rehearsal was just terrible. After it Mrs. Wy-

luda said, "Well, just remember that a bad dress rehearsal means a good performance. Please be here by
eight-thirty tomorrow. We go on at nine, before the
main service. I know you'll be wonderful."

Sure.

When I got home it was late afternoon and almost
dark. The house felt empty, and no one had turned
any lights on. I guessed everyone else had gone out,
and Grandmother was probably in her room; that
morning she had said she would lie low for the day
because she felt she was coming down with a cold —
which was no surprise, since we'd been soaked one
way or another almost every day during our nature
walks.

I wandered into the kitchen. The refrigerator was
filled with lamb and more asparagus and other veg-
etables for Easter dinner with the relatives, and there
were stick-on notes in Mom's handwriting attached
to things like cream and strawberries telling us not to
eat them. Mom does that around holidays. I found
an apple with no note on it and wandered into the
TV room. There was nothing going on, and I sat there
in the dark eating the apple.

I was just about to go up and wake Grandmother
when I heard the car drive up, and in a minute they
were at the door. Dad was carrying Sally all wrapped
up in a blanket. He was moving fast.

"What happened? What's wrong?" I said.

"Don't know," he answered over his shoulder,

going past me. "That's the problem." He struggled up the stairs. Mom and Pat came in. They had that white look around the eyes they both get when they're really worried.

"She woke up with a sore throat and a violent headache," Mom said, "and I took her temperature and she had a little fever, and then suddenly it shot up around noontime. It went so high we took her to Dr. Hayes at the hospital. They kept her forever, testing for this and that."

"They keep saying what it *isn't*," Pat said. "It isn't meningitis, it isn't mononucleosis, it isn't strep throat. Why can't they figure out what it *is*?"

"Well, since it didn't test out as any of those things, they had to figure it was some kind of flu," Mom said, taking off her coat. "But if her temperature gets any higher . . ." She looked so worried I got scared.

I went upstairs to Sally's room. Dad had got her settled in bed. "She's already asleep," he whispered. "The hospital really tuckered her out. I think she'll rest now for a while anyway." He took off his coat. "I'll take the first turn watching."

"Let me," I said. I suddenly didn't want to leave the room.

"All right," Dad said. "Thanks, Ned. I'll help Mom get some dinner together and check on Grandmother. Her cold is worse, too. Call me if anything changes in her breathing, or if she starts moving around a lot." He looked tired as he left the room. I brought a chair near Sally's bed and sat down.

She was breathing really fast, in and out so you could hear it. Her eyelids fluttered a little. Her face was flushed, like someone had put rouge makeup on it. The only light in the room came from her night-light, which Dad had flicked on. Ever since she was little, Sally's been afraid of the dark. It's funny in a way: here's this brainy kid who can play the violin better than almost anyone, but she has a pink rabbit night-light and keeps a huge bunch of stuffed animals. I mean, you wouldn't know she was some kind of a genius just from being around her or being her brother or something. I don't even think about it usually, except sometimes when I hear her play, or when she suddenly quotes practically a whole book at the dinner table. Most of the time she's just my little sister, and right now she looked so tiny curled up under the covers. I kept thinking of all the lousy things I'd said to her all week.

We took turns watching Sally until my parents made me go to bed. They said that tomorrow would be hectic enough, depending on how things went with Sally, but in any case I was to go to my play.

I woke up early, and for the first time all week the sun was shining. I stretched out my feet to feel the patch of sunlight on the floor before I remembered to check under the pillow for the new pair of socks that the Easter bunny usually puts there on Easter

Sunday — "to help us put our best foot forward in the spring," Mom says. I didn't expect to find any, but there they were — long white basketball socks with black and yellow bands on top. I put them on and sat for a minute, listening. It really was strange to be in a house that was dead quiet on Easter morning. Usually we'd all be up by now, rousted out by Sally, who would be gobbling the jelly beans in her Easter basket. No Easter baskets this year.

I walked down the hall to Sally's room. Dad was there in the chair by her bed. He had dozed off. Sally was still breathing like a rusty hinge. I walked as quietly as I could into my parents' bedroom so I wouldn't wake Mom, and slipped my hand under Dad's pillow and found a pair of dark blue socks. Somehow it seemed important to get them to him before he woke up. I walked back to Sally's room and put the socks on his knee. Sally still looked pretty flushed, and for a minute I wondered if I should wake Dad up, but she was breathing all right, so I left them and went downstairs.

It was completely quiet down there. Walking through the dining room on my way to the kitchen, I saw that the table was all pulled out and extra leaves added for the relatives. The table was set with a fancy white tablecloth with lace on it, and in the middle was a big china egg, painted with flowers and a big rooster on top, that only comes out at Eastertime.

Then in the kitchen, on the table, I found the Easter baskets. I couldn't believe it. Mom and Dad must have done them in the middle of the night between turns of watching Sally. For a minute it was like any other Easter, until the dead quiet reminded me that for Sally things didn't look that good at all. I took the basket with Sally's name on it and quietly went back upstairs and put it on her night table. Our house seemed dark as death, even though it was nice and sunny outside. By then it was almost eight, so I went out and got on my bike and headed downtown for the church.

I was glad no one from home was at the play, because the performance was just about as bad as you could imagine. A bad dress rehearsal means a good performance? That dress rehearsal must have been a whole lot better than it seemed at the time. First, when the curtain drew back, all the kids and their parents clapped before they realized that Vic, who had the first line, was talking. So nobody heard him but the first few rows, who giggled when he started over. Then Gail bumped heads with me when she leaned over to tuck in my laprobe, and the little kids in the front rows laughed again. In fact they laughed a lot, even though this was supposed to be a serious play. I sounded just as bitter and hopeless as Cedric is supposed to sound, but at one point I forgot a line and Mrs. Wyluda had to prompt me, and she did it so loud that some little kid in the front row repeated it and everyone laughed, including Vic, who was standing beside me. I wanted to sink through the floor.

The real killer came at the end. I was supposed to open the box that the fool cocoon had been hatching in just as the butterfly hatched out, and it was supposed to fly away. Mr. Hurd had rigged up a sort of wire thing that I was to hitch secretly to the plastic butterfly; he'd pull the wire offstage, so the butterfly would look like it was flying. Then I was supposed to stagger to my feet — the first time I'd got up out of the wheelchair on my own, right? — and take a step after the butterfly, and say, "Look! It's alive! It's alive! It's born! It can fly!" Well, that was the great moment of the play, as you can tell

What happened was that I forgot to hold up the blanket, so when I stood up and took a step toward the butterfly I stumbled and knocked into the wire. The wire broke, sproing! and the butterfly shot up into the air, boing! and then came spinning down and landed, thwack! a couple of feet ahead of me just as I said, "It's alive! It's alive!" I couldn't think of anything to do except pick it up and cradle it in my hands as if it was just having a bit of trouble flying. Then I gently chucked it out the window as I said the rest of my lines. I doubt if anyone heard them, though, with all the laughter in the place.

After this heartbreaking drama was finally over — when I took my bow, some kid shouted, "It's alive!

It's alive!" — we all went backstage to change and take off the makeup. Mrs. Wyluda brought back doughnuts and orange juice, and she and Mr. Hurd and the other kids' parents and brothers and sisters were milling around saying what a great job we'd done. No one seemed bothered by the butterfly fiasco. Nerd clapped me on the shoulder and said, "Good save, Ned?" — like I was a hockey goalie who maybe, but maybe not, had just stopped a penalty shot. The phone kept ringing and someone tipped over my paper cup of orange juice into the box of face powder.

Finally Mrs. Wyluda answered the phone, and out of half an ear I heard her say, "Oh, *no!* Oh, my dear! To the hospital?" I walked over closer. "Then there's real danger . . . ? Oh, Otis, I'm so sorry. Yes, I'll tell Ned to start back as soon as he gets his makeup . . ."

But I was already out of there and on my bike and pedaling like a madman by the time she finished the sentence.

It was like I had been waiting for the worst to happen. It couldn't happen, not to Sally, but now it was happening anyway and I couldn't stop it. There I had been fooling around with that damn butterfly, while Sally . . . Had she seen her Easter basket? Had she woken up at all? Was she in pain? How could you get a fever and die, just like that? And only yesterday I'd *hit* her!

At home I leapt off my bike, sending it into the

bushes, and burst through the front door and into the living room.

And there, sitting up on the sofa, wrapped in a blanket, her eyes open, was Sally.

"Hi, Ned," she said. Her voice sounded weak. "How did the play go?"

I just stared at her. I couldn't speak. Pat came into the room from the kitchen. I said, "What . . . what . . ."

"Boy, do you look dumb with makeup on," Pat said. "Did Sally tell you? Dad took Grandmother to the hospital. Her cold went into her chest and they're worried about pneumonia. She'll be all right, though. Mom's in the kitchen calling everybody to tell them."

I could hear my heart pounding. "I thought she was dead," I told Pat.

"Dead? Grandmother?"

"No. Sally."

"Sally? Oh, she's lots better. She'll be okay by Tuesday."

"Tuesday? What's Tuesday?"

"You know," Sally said. "The seder." She smiled weakly. "The famous seder? With all the famous people?"

I wiped the sweat off my forehead. Pat looked at me more closely. "Ned, are you okay?"

Okay? Is okay what you feel when someone lifts a huge rock off your chest? Is okay what you feel when the Angel of Death passes over your house? I felt like Cedric at the end of that stupid play. No, more like the butterfly. I felt like flying out the window.

"Yeah, I'm okay," I said, and collapsed on the sofa beside Sally.

"So how was the play?" she asked.

"Fine."

"I mean really."

"Really? Well, really it was awful. It was really a disaster. It was really terrible." I stood up on the sofa. "It was putrid. It stank. It was incredibly bad. It was the worst play ever!" By now I was jouncing up and down, flinging out my arms and legs. Sally was staring at me. "But we kept our socks up! We lent ourselves to the author!" Sally smiled. "We kept a stiff upper lip! We saved the day . . . !" Finally she was really laughing.

"Hallelujah!" I said. "Hallelujah!"

The Fabulous
Fourth

It HAD BEEN raining for three days and three nights. So far, the summer had been a bust. We were staying at Grandmother Scott's guest cottage on Cape Cod for the Fourth of July, like we always do, and I was bored. I had read all the books I could stand, there was no TV, I didn't know any kids in town, I was missing two games in my summer baseball league, and my sisters and I were at each other's throats. On the morning of July Fourth — another lousy day — we began playing Monopoly at eight-thirty in the morning and finished two minutes later when Pat said I was a cheater and I flipped the board over into her lap and she threw all her paper money in my face.

Mom came into the room and said, not too gently, "Sally, you go to the bunk room this instant and practice your violin. Pat, come in here and help me with the picnic. Ned, I want you to empty the garbage and every wastebasket in the house and then go take a walk or something. We'll meet you at the parade, unless it's pouring. *Get*, now, all of you."

So I stumped around doing all the trash and then walked out of the house and down to the town beach. Today wasn't raining. Today was fogging. No one was around except for a skinny old guy fishing from the middle of the dock. I walked out past him to the very end and looked out to sea as far as I could, which was about two feet because of the fog. They wouldn't hold the parade in this muck. I turned around and walked slowly back towards the beach. As I passed the skinny guy I noticed a puffer fish lying on the dock beside his tackle box. I turned around and kept walking backwards, hoping the fish would blow itself up, the way they do sometimes. That would be the high point of the week, I thought.

That's when I stepped backward off the dock.

I fell a long way straight down into shallow water, landing on my side. I could feel my left arm break, and it made a scary underwater sound: *kruck!* I swallowed a lot of seawater, and when I tried to crawl to my knees to get my head and shoulders out of the ocean, my right knee collapsed under me in pain. I fell back under and began drowning in about two feet of water.

Suddenly I was pulled clear by the collar of my

shirt. "What the devil you up to, boy?" It was the skinny fisherman. I don't know how he got down there so fast. He looked really mad. He pounded me on the back, and I said something like "Haghk! Gaghk!" He swore at me and called me a fool.

"What in hell's your name, boy?"

"A-Haghk! Ned! Gaghk! Scott!"

Then he put an arm like steel around my waist and hauled me into shore and up to an old Chevy. My left arm was numb. My whole body felt numb. The man yanked open the door, shoved me in, ran around to his side, got in, and drove like crazy to Grandmother Scott's house. There, he pulled me from the car again, marched me up the steps onto her big front porch, and pounded on her door with his fist like he was trying to break it down.

"Cynthia!" he said when she finally opened. "This'll be one of yours. He needs looking after."

"Why, thank you, Martin." Grandmother took a step or two out onto the porch. She was thinner since her illness at Eastertime, so that her big nose stuck out more. She stooped over her walking stick. Sometimes she really did remind me of a witch. "Ned?" she said. "Whatever happened?"

". . . I fell off the dock," I said.

"In heaven's name, how?"

"Well, I . . . d-don't know." My teeth were beginning to chatter. "I wasn't watching where I was going. I was just sort of buh . . . bored."

Behind me, the fisherman snorted.

"What?" Grandmother looked annoyed. She took another step toward me and leaned to look closer at my face. "Do you mean to tell me you fell off a dock because you were bored?" Her face seemed to grow bigger as I looked at it. It was blowing up just like a puffer fish. I swayed and fell down flat on the porch.

The next thing I knew, I was in the backseat of a car, lying on my back, my head in Grandmother's lap. She was looking down at me. My head was clear now, and my arm ached.

"I didn't notice your broken arm," Grandmother said, "for which I apologize." She didn't sound very sorry. "Martin didn't see it, either. He is being kind to drive us."

I lifted my head enough to see that Martin was the fisherman. In a low voice I said to Grandmother, "He was so mad at me. I thought he was going to kill me."

"And why shouldn't he be angry?" she said sharply, good and loud. "You scared the *wits* out of him, poor man." This lack of sympathy reminded me, just in case I needed it, how tough to take Grandmother Scott can be. You'd think she might feel sorry for a kid who'd just broken his arm on the Fourth of July, but no. She probably thought it was a weakness to show sympathy, or even to need it. Not that I did.

Martin drove us to the hospital, where they knocked me out with gas, and fixed the broken bone, and put a cast on my arm and a bandage on my right knee, which they said was just bruised and sprained. Afterward, we walked — I hobbled — back out to the car. Somewhere along the line it had turned into a really nice day. There was a bright blue sky and a little breeze that flapped the red, white, and blue flags strung across the front of the hospital. Grandmother and I got in the backseat again. She hadn't said a single word the whole time in the hospital. I wasn't sure if I felt sick to my stomach from the gas, or just hungry. Half of me was mad at everything, and the other half felt like crying. The fisherman started up the car without a word, and we headed back.

Grandmother turned to me. "Tell me, Ned," she said, like she was giving me an intelligence test, "are you still bored?"

I looked over at her. "What?"

"I said, are you still bored."

"Well . . ." I didn't know what she wanted. "I guess not," I said, and shrugged.

"You guess not. You're not sure."

"All right, I'm sure," I said. What I was sure of was that it was taking a long time to get home. I wondered if Grandmother had called Mom or Dad.

She leaned toward me a little. "No one answered the phone when I called from the hospital," she said, reading my mind. "I suppose they're at the parade, don't you think?"

I shrugged again. "I guess so," I said.

"Listen to me, Ned," Grandmother said. "Once upon a time there was a boy named Harwood Bridge-water who wanted to fly like a bird. This story will lose nothing if I tell you that Harwood Bridgewater was my brother, your great-uncle. When he was about your age he saw a drawing of a man with man-made wings. It fired his imagination. He decided to make wings of his own. Never mind that the drawing was hundreds of years old, and the wings hadn't worked then, either. Harwood's would work.

"So he cut a lot of canvas from an old army tent that his father had put in the attic. With some fishing line and a sailor's needle he stitched the canvas around some thin steel rods. He made shoulder sockets out of horsehair couch stuffing, and stitched the canvas around them, too. He made handgrips out of leather, and attached them to the underside of the canvas. When he finished he had something that looked vaguely like bat wings. Anyone in the world could see that they wouldn't work. The canvas was too heavy, and Harwood didn't know how to sew very well. His parents forbade him to try out the wings from anything higher than the stone wall in the garden.

"So one morning Harwood got up early and hauled his wings out to the highway, about two miles from your guest house. He waited there for someone in a truck to offer him a ride, and he got one, all the way to Provincetown. There, he carried his wings one by one up the Provincetown tower. You know that tower, of course. Have you been up it?"

"Yes."

"You find it high?"

"Yes."

"Indeed it is. And Harwood found a place at the top of it to jump from. He stood there holding his wings and looking down. He pictured himself leaping out into the air. He pictured the wings flapping and then failing, and the ground rushing up to meet him. He pictured himself lying on the ground in agony with many broken bones. Then he carried his wings back down the tower one by one and called his father to come pick him up. It was most humiliating. No one wanted to laugh at Harwood, but at dinner that night we got to talking about it, and then everyone did laugh, because, really, it was very funny.

"Early the next morning Harwood took his wings up to the attic and climbed with them out of a dormer window onto the roof. He stood on the edge of the roof and put on the wings. He leapt into the air. The wings flapped and failed. The ground rushed up to meet him. He broke an arm and a leg. They put a cast on his leg from the ankle to the hip, and on his arm from the shoulder to the wrist. Harwood was in a wheelchair for two weeks, then he used a single crutch for two more, then he limped around with a cane. But you know, in spite of discomfort, he was the proudest and happiest boy on Cape Cod."

She stopped. I looked at her face but she was staring straight ahead. I didn't know what I was supposed to say about her crazy brother who jumped off a roof with his stupid bat wings, so I said nothing. If I pulled a stunt like that, my parents would call in a shrink.

Suddenly from the front seat Martin said a swear that would have got me shut in my room, but Grandmother only said, "It's the parade, Martin. Main and High streets will be impossible. Try Court."

Martin swerved sharply to the right, muttering under his breath about summer people, and I swerved sharply to the left against my broken arm and tried not to yell.

Grandmother turned back to me. "You, of course," she said in a pleasant voice, "you think that it is better to break an arm by falling off a dock because you're bored and don't watch where you're going, than by flying."

"I didn't say that," I protested.

"No, you didn't."

There was a silence. Then she said, "What do you imagine boredom is, Ned?"

I shrugged. "Nothing to do, I guess."

"Oh, that's where you're wrong. Boredom isn't nothing to do, though that may come of it. Boredom is nothing to *think*. Boredom is a lack of independence."

Boredom is listening to this crapola with an arm

ache, a knee ache, a stomachache, and a headache, I thought, but kept quiet.

"What a good day this is," she went on, "for us to discuss these things. Independence Day. You do know what independence means?"

"Yes," I said. I decided I'd do better with Grandmother if I just said yes to everything.

"Then," she said, "you will understand this: a person who is independent can always think. A person who thinks can always do. People who are bored are not independent enough to think, and that's why they have nothing to do. Is that clear to you?"

"Yes."

She frowned at me, but then her forehead smoothed out and her mouth quirked up at the corners. "I see," she said. She patted my good knee. "I can see you are almost as clever as you think you are, but there's no matter. We'll find time."

Time for what? Was that a threat? I turned from her and looked out the window. What did she want from me? She really was a witch. We drove past familiar houses and the salt marsh, and I couldn't wait to get home. To tell you the truth, I did think it would be nice to get a little sympathy from someone, and maybe something cold to drink.

But it was to her house that the fisherman drove, not the guest cottage. I had forgotten that no one would be home.

"I'll call over in a little while," she said as we

pulled up in front of her house. "But I think I shall keep you with me. You are in no condition to go to the fireworks tonight, much less the three-legged race this afternoon. Besides," she added as she opened the car door, "there are other stories you should hear about independence and broken bones." That seemed to strike her as funny, and she laughed. "Thank you, Martin," she said as she got out of the car.

The fisherman turned around from the front seat, leaned back, and pulled the door handle on my side. "Allow me," he said. He had a mean smile. "No need to bore you."

What had I *done?* It wasn't enough to break an arm and sprain a knee, no, I had to take all this abuse! I got out and slammed the door behind me with my good hand.

"You're welcome," he said, and drove off.

"Follow me," said Grandmother in her bossy way, and she walked up the porch steps and into her house, stumping along with her cane more quickly than I could without one.

"Sit right there," she said when I entered, pointing to a straight-backed chair at her dining room table. The house was dark and cool and smelled like cloves, maybe from the pink flowers in the middle of the dark shiny table. Grandmother went to the kitchen, and returned in a few minutes with a big bowl. She plunked it down in front of me.

"Eat this," she said, and sat down across from

me, her arms folded on the table in front of her. I looked down into the bowl. It was vanilla ice cream with strawberries on top. I couldn't believe it. I looked up at Grandmother in confusion. She was frowning.

"Once upon a time," she said, "there was a young man so beloved, so well-favored, and so rich that he might have died of boredom save for a freak accident. This story will lose nothing if I tell you that the man was David Otis Scott, my husband and your grandfather. Go ahead, eat your ice cream."

I looked down at the bowl, then back up at her. I didn't know what was going on. I took a spoonful of the ice cream. I put it in my mouth. It tasted great. I ate it while she talked.

She cleared her throat. "Your grandfather grew up rich, a little arrogant, and a little bored. When he turned twenty-one he inherited a large fortune. The year was 1929. Do you know what the Great Depression was?"

"Yes."

She raised her eyebrows. "Do you. Then you know that many rich people lost their money in it. Your grandfather was one of them, and he lost his in a spectacular way. During the first week of the crash, the worst week in the financial history of this country, your grandfather was on a pleasant October cruise along Cape Hatteras. He knew that there might be some difficulties on Wall Street, but, as I say, he was a little arrogant and a little bored, and he had never spent much time watching where he was going. He took with him his cousin Christian and their lawyer, a friend named Joseph Stern, and two cases of a wine called Château Montrose, which had cost him almost half as much as the boat they were all sailing in. No one was left at home who had the power of attorney for your grandfather. Do you know what power of attorney means?"

"Yes."

She gave me a look.

"I mean basically," I added, swallowing ice cream. "Sort of."

"I see." She narrowed her eyes. "Well, to cut short a long and exciting sea yarn, they were taken up by a vicious storm and blown halfway to the Caribbean and back. Their engine failed, the mainsail was blown to shreds, and they had to use a spinnaker just to avoid capsizing in the heavy seas. Great fish were swept on deck. I won't bore you with these details. But you might be interested to know that at one point the mainmast broke, striking your grandfather, and it broke his forearm in three places. And all the while, even as he fought for his life at sea, his money back home was melting away like snow in summer. Yet when the boat finally limped safely back to Virginia Beach, where his brother waited on the dock to tell him exactly how much his voyage had cost, your grandfather went down on his knees, right there on the dock with his mangled arm, and kissed the salty boards! Any news was good news, you see. Life itself was all that was precious to him now. He knew that his own choice had ruined him financially, but he had survived an incredible adventure. And the wonderful part is that his zest for life never changed. He was a remarkably independent man the rest of his life, adventurous and good-natured through thick and thin, though he never gained much of his money back."

She stopped talking. Everything was quiet except for a bee or two, and the distant sound of firecrackers going off now and then. The ice cream was gone. My arm and leg hurt.

"So," she said, still looking across the table at me. "What do you make of all that?"

"Yes" didn't seem like a good enough answer, so I said, "I don't know," which was the truth. I shifted in my chair. "I mean, what do you *want* me to make of it?"

"What do I want? Why, for you to listen, I suppose." She smiled, but her eyes looked sad, and for a moment I thought I might have hurt her feelings. "You may have noticed that I'm an old woman. I may not have all that much time left to tell you these family fables." She pushed herself up from the table. "Speaking of families, I'd better try to call your father."

She went over to the phone and dialed. If I had hurt her in some way, I couldn't tell it by looking at her back, which was as straight as the backs of the chairs around her table. Even if she wasn't exactly sympathetic, I didn't want to hurt her. I just wanted to go home.

Mom and Dad and my sisters had just got back from the parade, and when Grandmother told them what had happened, they came right over.

Talk about sympathy! Dad said, "Good Lord, Ned, you could have broken your neck! What a frightening fall! Thank God Martin was there. Did I ever tell you about the time he cut a fishhook out of my thumb?" And Mom said she wished she'd just sent me to my room, that the fight was equally my sisters' fault, and on and on. Pat was okay, she didn't say anything much, except that she was sorry, and the parade wasn't much this year. But Sally gets wound up pretty quick about accidents and stuff, and she was almost crying. "Are you gonna be okay? I mean really? Does it hurt a lot? You want some aspirins or something?"

While they were all fussing over me I noticed Grandmother standing off to the side with a little smile on her face. That made me mad, but I was embarrassed at how my family was babying me. After all, I wasn't *that* badly hurt. I finally said, "Look, I'm fine; it's just a little break; come on now, let's go home." And I got up from my chair, completely forgetting about my knee. When I stepped out with that leg, it buckled again and I went down on the floor. Confusion broke out all over the place. Sally yelled and Pat ran to lift me up too quickly and hurt my arm, Dad shouted, "Leave it! Leave it!" and Mom said, "Oh, *dear!*"

No kidding, it was a total botch.

"I really do think it unwise," Grandmother said when I got back into my chair, "to take him to the fireworks tonight."

"I wouldn't think of it!" Dad said.

"And aren't you going to a cocktail party beforehand?"

"That's true," Mom said to Dad.

"He can be made perfectly comfortable here for the night."

"Of *course* he can. That would be wonderful, Mother," Dad said.

"Thank Grandmother, dear," Mom reminded me, and I gritted my teeth, and said, "Thank you, Grandmother."

"I shall serve us all some lemonade," Grandmother said, "and after that, you all go on about your business, and perhaps Ned will feel up to family doings tomorrow."

I could feel the trap closing. When Grandmother went for the lemonade, I leaned over and said to Mom and Dad, "I don't *want* to stay here for the night!"

"Lousy luck it happened today, Ned," Dad said. "But I really think that's the best plan."

"Don't forget, dear," Mom said just before the lemonade came, "Grandmother Scott is getting old now. I think sometimes she's a little lonely. And you really will be better off here. Do you mind so much staying? We'll run across before bed to say good-night."

"No, I guess not," I said. What else was there to say? After the lemonade and some great homemade brownies, they all left to get ready for the party and fireworks.

I guess I must have looked pretty bummed out, because Grandmother said, "I am sorry about the fireworks, Ned. I remember that they are the best part. Here, I'll leave your grandfather's walking stick against your chair. When you're ready, go on into the living room. That big leather chair with the hassock will be good for your leg. I have a few things to see to. You know where the facilities are for washing up."

Since I had to go to the bathroom anyway, I decided to keep on going into the living room and check out the old chair. A few minutes after I got there she came in with a radio and a book with an old green cover.

"This was one of your father's favorites. *The Thirty-nine Steps.* Perhaps it will pass the time. It has been an eventful day. I shall take a rest now. Are you comfortable?"

I wasn't, and I certainly wasn't going to act all nice and happy just because she'd given me some new toys, but I said, "Yes," keeping to my earlier answering style. I left the book and the radio where she'd put them and just sat there. The curtains were partly drawn, so the room was kind of dark, with beams of sunlight shining through those red vases she has up on the window ledges. I guess I must have dozed off, because the next thing I knew, the sunlight was gone and Grandmother's voice came at me from the side, surprising me.

"You are awake. I'm glad you could sleep a bit. The doctor said you should take these after six hours." She held out a couple of pills and a glass of water. I was dying of thirst. My arm ached like hell and I wanted out. I was glad that Grandmother left the room right away, in case I might be about to feel like crying or something. But then I was okay. Really. I just sort of sat there in the half dark, wondering what her next move would be. But what she did next was bring me practically my favorite food: a hamburg (cut up so I could eat with my one arm), mashed potatoes swimming in butter, and peas. There was a huge piece of chocolate cake on another plate. The milk was ice-cold. She pulled up a chair nearer to mine and sat there while I ate, saying nothing at all. I began to get a little nervous.

"Do you like your dinner?" she said after a while.

"Yes," I said. But that really did sound rude, so I quickly added, "Hamburgers are my favorite food."

"I should be giving you salmon and peas on the Fourth. But I thought you might need something more familiar to mend your bones. Young bones mend well.

Old bones not so well. Take your great-grandfather's cousin Elmer Geiger from Kentucky. His bones never did mend. I believe it was because of boredom that they didn't. Boredom infected them, you could say. Indeed, he died of boredom."

Grandmother hitched her chair right up to mine and reached to adjust my tray. The diamonds and rubies on her bony fingers flashed in the light of the candle she'd lighted on the table. I wondered if she'd turn on a light, or if we would sit all night in the dark. I kept on chewing away.

"Elmer was bored all his life long," she said. "When he was your age, he slept twelve hours a day. In high school he made good marks but was interested in nothing. He was bored in college and very bored in law school. As a lawyer he made a great deal of money working for businesses that bored him. He married a nice girl but paid no attention to her, and he thought the two pretty children she gave him were a terrible bother. Elmer was bored with wars and poverty and injustice. He was bored with golf and picnics and dances.

"As the years went by, he began to understand that he wasn't very happy. Well, he would fix that, he finally decided. He took up deep-sea diving, and mountain climbing, and hang-gliding. He threw himself into these excitements. Was there a new plane to be tested? Up he flew. Was there a dangerous jungle to be explored? Off he went. He spent less and less time with his family. In fact, they often didn't know where he was.

"One day when he was forty-two he up and joined a small circus that was passing through town. Truth to tell, he *bought* the circus; it was the only way he could join it at his age. He began to train on the tightrope. He never used a safety net.

"Well, one day in a small town in Wisconsin, the center pole of his main tent cracked in a strong wind. Elmer was on the high wire at the time. He heard the pole crack and looked over. He didn't watch where he was going. He fell to his death. I imagine he must have broken just about every bone in his body."

I looked up at her quickly from my plate of cake. I was pleased to catch her in a mistake. "You said he died of boredom," I said.

"Why, so he did," she answered. "He was in the *habit* of being bored, don't you see. By the time he tried to change, it was too late. Certain people have got to wake up early if they're going to wake up at all, Ned. They've got to watch where they're going, starting *right now*."

She leaned forward as she said this, and I put my fork down and stared right back at her. Oh, I saw where she was headed, all right. I saw right through her story about Elmer. Here I was, still feeling lousy, and my own grandmother was trying to make me feel worse by telling me I was like some jerk I never even met.

"I don't go falling off docks *all* the time, you know," I said.

She lifted her eyebrows. "I should hope not."

"What I mean is, I'm not bored a lot, except sometimes when it rains. I don't sleep twelve hours a day. I like school. I know I did something stupid, and now I've got a broken arm. That's all there is to it. You know?"

She nodded, a little smile on her face. "Yes, I know. And I must say, that's a much better response than saying 'yes' all the time."

"But why are you making such a big deal out of this?"

"Well, you're immobile right now — a captive audience," she said with a laugh. "I thought these family fables might entertain you." She paused and gave a small sigh. "But the real reason, I suppose, is that you are my grandson, my family. Your character matters a great deal to me. I want to be sure that the family matters to you."

This caught me by surprise, and I didn't know what to say. I thought about her stories again. Finally, I said, "I can understand why your brother had to try out his wings no matter what." She nodded. "And I can see why Grandfather might see things differently after he almost got killed or drowned."

"Yes. But?"

"But Elmer's life doesn't sound so boring to me."

Grandmother nodded. "He experienced a lot of

excitement, it's true. But I believe he depended on those things to distract him from the real problem."

"What was that?"

"His mind never developed," she said. "He tried to do what others in his family had done, but he never understood himself. He grew up, but he was never independent."

"So you mean, after a while everything bored him?"

"I believe so, yes."

"And then he had to keep trying more and more exciting things, I guess."

"That's exactly right. But since he never knew why he did what he did, he was never satisfied."

"I can understand that," I said. I looked at her. "But it's hard to do your own thing when your family's always telling you what to do. Poor guy."

"Yes. It *is* hard. Poor guy indeed."

We sat there for a while without speaking. Then she said, "Do you think you could make it up a lot of stairs with that knee? I believe it would be worth it if you could."

I thought she meant to go to bed, and I said sure. I was pretty tired. I reached for the book.

"Ah. I'm glad you'll give the book a try," she said, "but leave it now. You'll need your good hand to get to the widow's walk."

She'd surprised me again. Grandmother's house has a flat lookout place on the roof, called a widow's walk, where sailors' wives used to watch for their husbands to come back safe to shore. We weren't allowed to go up there, it wasn't safe. But we always wanted to. I'd given up asking, but Sally still asked every summer.

"Yes," Grandmother said, reading my mind. "It isn't safe, really, for active children. But for an old crock like me and a temporary cripple like you, it's safe enough this one night of the year."

We both got up. I felt sort of shaky, but I said, "You better take Grandfather's stick to help you."

"Thank you, Ned, but I have another right here. I'd like you to have that one to keep." She started off before I had a chance to thank her, and I hobbled to catch up.

It was hard walking up three flights of stairs, but luckily Grandmother had to go slow, too. "Both of our doctors would have me drawn and quartered for this," she said as we rested on the third floor landing.

Grandmother unlocked the door to the roof with a big iron key, and we went up a twisting iron stairway that was almost like a ladder. When we got to the widow's walk, she found a couple of canvas chairs for us to sit on. It felt good to sit down.

It was beautiful up there on the roof. We sat up high and still. The moon and stars were near, and the sounds of the earth seemed way below us.

"Sally would really like it up here," I said, for some reason — the words just popped out.

"You wish she were here with us?"

"No." I was sure of that. I was glad to have Grandmother to myself. "She just came into my head, is all. *She* has an independent mind."

"So do you, Ned, I'm glad to say."

I looked over at her, sitting beside me in the near dark. She was smiling at me. I smiled back.

"So do you, Grandmother," I told her.

Then the fireworks started out over the bay, sharp crackles and echoing booms, big splashes of diamonds and rubies, fading to ghost tracks against the sky.